They were moving towards the back door when a bolt of lightning startled the life out of Joel. He was turning as it happened, and a flicker of movement caught the corner of his eye. He gripped his sister's arm urgently. 'Cassie, did you see that?'

'OK, that would be this stuff that we call lightning—'

'Over there!' A running figure, too slim and slight to be Damon, and entirely the wrong build for Tim. He was tearing away as though he thought someone was after him.

'I didn't see anything.' Cassie turned round wildly. 'What? Over where?'

'There's someone in the garden.'

Praise for *The Intruders*:

'A ghoulish little book' *Irish Times*

'written in a clear prose style with enough characterisation to make you care for the protagonists . . . should give young adults the collywobbles the minute they turn off their bedside light' *SFX Magazine*

'*The Devil's Footsteps* established E. E. Richardson as a horror writer with an uncanny grasp of the human psyche. With *The Intruders*, Richardson further asserts her considerable powers as writer and social commentator . . . the success of this novel's horror arises through the clever interplay of paranormal activities and familial discord' *Achuka*

'Modern horror at its scariest' *Writing Magazine*

'E. E. Richardson's skill in *The Intruders* is to tell a chilling ghost story firmly rooted in well-observed 21st-century family turmoil . . . a riveting page-turner' *TES*

Also by E. E. Richardson

The Devil's Footsteps
The Summoning

E . E . RICHARDSON

The Intruders

CORGI

THE INTRUDERS
A CORGI BOOK 978 0 552 55261 5

First published in Great Britain by The Bodley Head,
an imprint of Random House Children's Books

The Bodley Head edition published 2006
Corgi edition published 2007

1 3 5 7 9 10 8 6 4 2

Corgi Books are published by Random House Children's Books,
61–63 Uxbridge Road, London W5 5SA,
a division of The Random House Group Ltd,
in Australia by Random House Australia (Pty) Ltd,
20 Alfred Street, Milsons Point, Sydney, NSW 2061, Australia,
in New Zealand by Random House New Zealand Ltd,
18 Poland Road, Glenfield, Auckland 10, New Zealand,
in South Africa by Random House (Pty) Ltd,
Isle of Houghton, Corner Boundary Road & Carse O'Gowrie,
Houghton 2198, South Africa,
and in India by Random House India Pvt Ltd,
301 World Trade Tower, Hotel Intercontinental Grand Complex,
Barakhamba Lane, New Delhi 110001, India

THE RANDOM HOUSE GROUP Limited Reg. No. 954009
www.**kids**at**randomhouse**.co.uk

A CIP catalogue record for this book is available from the British Library.

Printed and bound in Great Britain by
Cox & Wyman Ltd, Reading, Berkshire

For Sam and Tara

'There it is!' Joel Demetrius leaned across his sister to point through the car window. 'Look, Cass, that's the house.'

At this distance, through the trees, you could see the size of the place but not the state of it. The peeling paint was invisible in the shadowed glimpses between tree trunks; the gaps in the slate roof were camouflaged by the mottling of age and moss. To Joel it looked huge and fascinating, a marked departure from the near-identical yellow-brick houses they'd been passing for most of the journey.

Cassie shrugged sullenly, and sank deeper into the car seat. 'So?'

'So . . . there it is.' Joel had decided he wasn't going to let his sister bring him down, but it wasn't proving an easy vow to keep. She'd been determinedly hating every moment of the trip so far, and they hadn't even got to the part she was unhappy about yet.

'I can't believe we have to share a house with *them*,' Cassie grumbled, low but just loud enough to be sure that Mum heard from the driver's seat. His older sister had never been shy about making her opinions known, and when it was snarled in that tone of voice, 'them' could mean only one thing: Gerald Wilder and his two sons. Or, as Cassie preferred to think of them, the intruders.

It had been just the two of them and Mum for as far back as Joel's memory would stretch. Cassie claimed to remember their father, but she was only a year older so that couldn't mean much: he'd walked out on them so early that Joel wouldn't have known the man's face if it hadn't been for photographs. If his sister missed their father more than he did, she was certainly in no hurry to replace him. So far as she was concerned, the three of them were just fine together, and the rest of the world could take a hike. *Especially* those parts of the world containing Gerald Wilder.

Joel didn't really mind Gerald. It was weird to have him around, weirder still for Mum to be engaged to him, but he seemed to be an all right sort of guy. Joel had gradually got used to him. Cassie hadn't, and she didn't want to try. She hated Gerald, she hated his kids even more, and she hadn't stopped screaming about it since she'd found they were moving in together. Unfortunately for her, it was from Mum that she'd inherited that stubborn streak, and she was definitely fighting a losing battle. Joel just wished she'd give it up and surrender gracefully.

He was actually quite looking forward to it all. Their old flat had been tiny, too cramped even when they were kids, never mind now they were both in their teens. Gerald had found this battered old place through his work in the building trade, and even though it would be like living on a construction site for the first few months, it would be worth it just to have so much space.

'Come on, Cassie!' Joel urged. 'The place is

massive! We could probably live there for, like, a year, and never even have to see them.'

He was exaggerating, and only trying to stir Cassie out of her gloom, but their mother shot him a stern glance in the rear-view mirror. 'Joel, don't you start as well,' she warned. 'One attitude problem in this car is already one too many. The Wilders are a part of this family now whether you like it or not, and you are *going* to be nice to them.'

'You can't make me,' Cassie muttered, slumping down in her seat. 'I didn't ask to come. You can't make it sound like I owe them something when I didn't even want to come.'

'Cassandra Demetrius, that will do! It's about time you got over yourself, young lady. Gerald is a perfectly nice man, and he has two lovely children, and if I say you're getting along with them – you're getting along with them.' Their mother had been uncharacteristically anxious about the pair of them taking to Gerald and his family, but her patience only stretched so far.

'*Lovely?* Them?' Cassie scoffed in disbelief. 'Have you *met* them?'

'Cassie. Stop it!' Their mother's voice had reached the warning level. For a moment Joel was afraid his sister would push it anyway, but she subsided and went back to staring moodily out of the window.

They pulled up in the big driveway, and piled out of the car. Joel roamed the front garden, glad of the chance to stretch his legs, but Cassie only had disapproving eyes for the shabby white van that was already parked there. 'They're here,' she said in a gloomy voice.

Their mother chose to ignore the tone. 'Yes, they are,' she said brightly. 'Gerald's been working really hard to get this place in a fit state to live in, so maybe you should be a little nicer to him. Now, if one of you two would like to run round the back and tell them we've arrived—'

'I'll do it,' Joel volunteered quickly. It wouldn't go well if Cassie was ordered to do it.

They'd been told to use the back door, because the imposing front entrance had seized up and was going to need some oiling. For all that it was stuck shut, it didn't make much of a barrier, since the wooden porch was so warped and rotten it wouldn't have taken much effort to tear a hole in it.

No would-be thief had bothered to make that effort – it was obvious from the most cursory glance that the house had been long abandoned. The paint was peeling, the wood was rotting, and almost everything that could crack, sag or fall off had already done so. All the same, the house retained a certain grandeur that the effects of age hadn't erased. Joel thought it was a sad sight, like seeing someone who'd become a shadow of their former self after years of hardship.

Cassie was not nearly so inclined to be charitable. 'Jeez, what a *dump*,' she said, shaking her head in disgust.

'It just needs a little work,' their mother said, with perhaps a tad too much optimism.

Joel jogged round the side along the gravel path, marvelling at the size of the grounds. Never mind a garden, this was practically a private park – you could have played a decent game of football out the back if it hadn't been so overgrown.

He didn't mind the chaos – wilderness beat a neatly cut lawn and boring flowerbeds any day. The same went for the house: it might be old and battered and perhaps a bit creepy with all those blank windows staring down, but at least it was *interesting*. It could have been so cool moving in here – if it hadn't been for Cassie spoiling everything.

The back door stood open, and Joel poked his head in cautiously. 'Hello?' He was instantly hit by the musty smell: like the house had been rolled up and kept at the bottom of a wardrobe for a couple of years. That would drive Mum crazy, he knew. She'd be off on a rampage with the air freshener before they'd even finished unpacking. Which would probably make it even harder to breathe. He hoped none of those windows were stuck shut.

He felt strangely uncomfortable just walking in the door like this. Joel knew this house was supposed to be his home now, but it didn't feel that way – any more than Mum and Gerald deciding they should be a family suddenly magically formed them into one. The yellowing walls and cracked ceiling seemed to belong to another age entirely, and he couldn't quite shake off the sensation of disapproving eyes peering at him from the shadows, waiting to see if this young invader would realize his mistake and leave, or would need to be forcibly ejected.

'Joel!' Gerald entered from the next room, smiling and wiping his hands on a towel. He was a tall, muscular man, with a mass of messy blond hair that surrounded his head like a scraggly halo. 'Is your mum out the front?'

He nodded, feeling suddenly shy as he always did around his soon-to-be-stepdad. 'And Cassie.' He didn't mind Gerald, but it was strange just having him around, let alone coming to live with him. He was supposed to be as good as family now, but Joel still felt like he had to put on his best behaviour as he would for a total stranger.

Gerald pulled a concerned face. 'Is she still sulking?'

'Yup.' Joel gripped the edge of the kitchen worktop nervously, and wished there was a way to make his sister give the Wilder family more of a chance.

'She'll get over it soon enough,' Gerald decided optimistically. Joel wasn't at all sure he was right.

Cassie showed no signs of getting over it as Gerald came out to help them unpack. She deliberately turned her back as he gave their mother an enthusiastic hug, and completely ignored his attempts at a friendly greeting. Joel, as usual, was left to babble and fill the silences before Gerald felt awkward or Mum got mad.

It had always been like that; Cassie was the fiery, quick-tempered one, and Joel had to be peacemaker. He hated it sometimes. He was the youngest – why should he always have to be the sensible one?

That was one reason he'd liked the idea of having stepbrothers: maybe one of *them* could be the grown-up for a change. The oldest, Damon, was a year older than Cassie; he could be the big brother, and Joel could hang out with Tim and do what he wanted instead of being sensible all the time. Except it hadn't worked out that way, because Cassie hated Damon even more than she hated Gerald.

'Where are the boys, Gerry?' asked their mother, as they tugged the heavy suitcases out of the boot.

'Inside, getting settled in.' He turned to Cassie and Joel. 'I moved your stuff into two of the bedrooms, but that's only temporary if you want to switch later. At the moment the boys are in together, but it's a little cramped for Damon, so I was thinking if Joel wouldn't mind sharing . . .'

Joel was opening his mouth to say that sounded

all right – he got on fine with Tim, and it might be fun to be able to talk in the middle of the night and things – but Cassie cut him off. 'Joel's going to stay next to me, so we can hang out together.' The words 'and without *your* kids' went unspoken, but everybody knew they were there anyway.

He really wouldn't have minded sharing a room, but he didn't want to upset Cassie either. 'Yeah, I'll just stay next to Cassie,' he said. 'Tim'd probably rather share with Damon than me, anyway.'

Gerald looked disappointed, but covered it quickly. 'OK, of course. If that's what you want.'

'OK. Can we see our rooms now?' asked Joel excitedly.

Gerald smiled at his enthusiasm. 'Go ahead. Your mother and I can finish unpacking from here. You two mind those stairs now. I had to take up the old carpet tiles because they were rotting, and there might still be some nails in there.'

'We will!' He dashed away, Cassie following.

'Oh, thank God,' she sighed dramatically, as they went in through the kitchen door. 'I thought we were *never* going to get away.'

'You should give Gerald a chance,' Joel advised her. 'He's OK. Really.'

'I don't care if he's Mother Teresa,' scowled Cassie. 'He's not ours. He's not *family*. Mum shouldn't keep pretending like he is, like we've got to accept him.'

'She's going to marry him next year,' Joel pointed out.

'If she does, I'm leaving home,' Cassie growled.

Joel was pretty sure she was exaggerating. Apart from anything else, where would she go? Mum was the only living family they had. Maybe that was why Cassie was so determined not to share her.

'Let's look at the rooms,' he said, changing the subject. 'I hope mine's got a window that looks out over the back garden.'

'I hope mine's as far away from *them* as possible.'

The master bedroom downstairs was the biggest, but the three on the upper floor were not exactly small. The Wilder boys' shared room was on the right, while his and Cassie's stuff had been moved into the two on the left of the landing. That was it for the upper floor, although a large square hatch in the ceiling of the hallway suggested there was some kind of loft space above.

The house had only one bathroom, but it was easily twice the size of the one back in the flat. There was even a door in the kitchen that Gerald said led down to a cellar. After their old home, it seemed like a mansion – but Cassie was still unimpressed. 'It's a stupid house. It's got stupid Gerald and his stupid kids, and I don't see how you can care about the rooms when *they're* here.'

Joel was getting pretty tired of the same old rant. 'Well, we're here too,' he snapped. 'So you might as well get used to it. We're here, so are they, and none of us are going anywhere.'

Joel fell in love with his new room instantly. It dwarfed the one he'd had back in the flat, making all his transplanted furniture look rather small and sad. The windows were huge, taking up half the wall, and they did indeed look out over the back garden. It was all rather shabby and extremely dusty, but that didn't bother him.

Cassie was much less easy to please. 'Look at it,' she sneered. 'It's a hellhole! All the walls are cracked, and it's so *dirty*—'

'Since when did you care?' Joel wanted to know. Cassie had never been a prissy, fussy kind of sister.

At school she was a bit of a brain, but she'd always been up for a game of kickaround football down at the park, or any kind of activity that got their mother grimacing over the state of their clothes. He'd been hoping that this summer they could actually have a good time in a house that had its own garden, but it looked like Cassie was going to spend the whole time finding things to hate about it.

'This sucks,' she told him moodily. 'We should've stayed in London.'

Joel shrugged. 'Think of it as an adventure,' he suggested.

'An adventure?' She raised an eyebrow. 'Aren't they supposed to be *fun*?'

Joel shrugged again. 'Looks like an adventure to me. You got, um, you got your castle, you got your jungle' – he waved towards the overgrown back garden – 'you got your monsters' – he gestured in the general direction of the Wilder boys' room, and that made Cassie giggle.

'Yeah. Monsters. Slimy, scummy, disgusting monsters.' But she was grinning. 'Think Mum would go mad if I slew them?'

14

'Yeah, probably.' Joel grinned back, pleased to have got his sister back into a more cheerful mood. 'Anyway, you're supposed to be the damsel in distress. You've got to wait for a handsome prince to come and rescue you.'

Cassie gave a very unladylike snort. 'Screw that! Any handsome prince comes riding up, I'll kick him in the kneecaps and nick his horse. And then I can get the hell out of here.'

'You can't ride a horse,' he reminded her.

'Sure I could! I could if I wanted to. I just never tried before, that's all.' She chewed her lower lip thoughtfully. 'I wonder if anyone round here keeps horses.'

Of course, no sooner had Joel succeeded in actually getting a halfway optimistic thought out of his sister than Gerald had to spoil it by yelling up the stairs that dinner was ready. A familiar frown began to darken her features, and he had to remind her, 'Bring your sword and shield, in case the monsters attack at dinner.'

'Hi, Joel.' Tim Wilder beamed at him across the table. Tim was about eighteen months younger than him, pudgy and very shy. He had scruffy blond hair like his father, but where Gerald was a big, imposing man, his son looked very young for his age.

The older brother, Damon, didn't really look like either of them. Joel supposed he must take after his mother; he had something of his father's height, but with dark brown hair and fine features. He had a brilliant smile, although it could as easily be cruelly mocking as friendly. He'd been OK to Joel, but Cassie's sullen attitude clearly rubbed him up the wrong way. Of course, his sarcastic jabs only made Cassie even more spiky . . . Putting Damon and his sister in the same room was never a good idea.

There was quite a contrast between the Wilder clan and their own little family. Though Tim was the only one who really qualified as plump, all three were fairly solidly built, while Cassie and Joel were slim and graceful like their mother. Cassie looked a lot like her, with dark coffee-coloured skin and shoulder-length braided hair. Joel was a little shorter than his sister, and wore his hair closely cropped. Nobody, stepping into the room, would have had the slightest difficulty in picking out which kid belonged to which family.

However, the point was that they were supposed to become one big happy family together. And that hadn't shown too many signs of happening yet.

Cassie took her place silently but resentfully, saving a particularly nasty glare for Damon. He pulled a face right back at her, but winked at Joel. Joel just sort of smiled at them all, not wanting to get into a fight with Cassie by being too friendly.

Things could have been strained but OK – if their parents hadn't been so determined to *force* them all into polite conversation. 'So – Cassie, Joel,' said Gerald, in a deliberately cheerful tone. 'What do you think of the house?'

'It's pretty cool.' Joel spoke up quickly. 'I like my room. And I love the garden.'

Of course, that wasn't good enough for their mother. 'Cassie?' she asked pointedly.

Mum! He wanted to bite through his fork in frustration. Why? Why did she have to do this? She *knew* Cassie wasn't going to suddenly be friendly and polite, so why did she have to keep *prodding* all the time?

Of course, if he were Cassie, he would have yelled that out loud like he wanted to. But no, he was Joel, the quiet, polite, well-behaved one. So he carried on eating, and tried not to wince too much as Cassie shrugged indifferently.

'What's that, Cassie? Didn't quite hear you there.'

Cassie shot her mother a sullen look and shrugged again. 'It's a house. What d'you want me to say?'

'Oh, don't sound *too* enthusiastic,' sniped Damon from the other side of the table. She sneered at him.

'Cassie Demetrius, what have I told you about pulling faces?'

'Um . . . *your face'll stick like that?*' she said innocently.

Gerald tried to defuse the situation by acting amused, but Cassie just shot him a look full of contempt.

'Who'd notice?' Damon muttered quietly to his plate.

Unfortunately, Cassie heard him. 'Hey!'

'Cassie! Simmer down,' their mother ordered.

'He started it.'

'And I'm finishing it. If you can't be nice, then keep your mouth shut.'

'How am I supposed to eat?'

18

'Starve yourself to death, do us all a favour,' suggested Damon. Cassie shrieked something angry, and it was Gerald's turn to rein in his oldest child.

'*Damon*. Apologize.'

Damon flashed her an insincere smile. 'Sorry,' he said lightly.

Their mother gave Cassie a nudge. 'Cassie, say sorry.'

'Yeah, whatever.' She turned her attention back to the meal, pretending Gerald and his sons weren't even there. Joel suddenly didn't have much of an appetite, but he was forced to stay in his seat and finish dinner anyway. They passed the rest of the meal in awkward, sulky silence. Part of the way through, Tim caught his eye and smiled sympathetically.

'Cassie – help with the washing up,' their mother ordered, when they were all finished.

Cassie looked aggrieved. 'Why am *I* the one who gets punished? It was him too,' she objected, jerking her head at Damon.

Their mother rubbed her forehead, the way she always did when Cassie was giving her a headache. 'It's not a punishment, Cassie. I'm just asking you for

19

a *little* bit of help. A tiny, *tiny* bit of co-operation. Do you think you can maybe cope with that?'

'Whatever.' Cassie shot a scowl at the triumphantly grinning Damon, and stomped after their mother into the kitchen.

As soon as the table was cleared, Joel shut himself away in his room, dug out his CD player and turned the volume up high. He closed his eyes and tried to pretend that the rest of the world didn't exist.

He was doing quite well at it too, until an almighty screech from Cassie's room shook the entire household.

Joel yanked the headphones out of his ears and bolted for his sister's room. He came to an abrupt halt in the doorway, amazed by the chaos inside.

Cassie had left her suitcase full of clothes on the bed when they went down for dinner. Now, though, the suitcase had been flung open and her things thrown all over the room. Crumpled T-shirts littered the floor and balled-up socks were scattered everywhere, as if someone had been playing football with them.

'Cassie, what happened?' he asked, jaw dropped.

It was a stupid question, but he couldn't think of a better one.

Damon suddenly skidded up behind him, looking alarmed. 'What's going on?' he demanded.

Cassie pointed an accusing finger at him. '*You,*' she said, in a dark tone that sounded frighteningly like their mother when she was just on the verge of losing it.

Damon peered through the doorway, and his eyebrows rose. 'Whoa, what happened to your room?'

Cassie stared at him. 'What *happened*? Come on, you really think I'm going to fall for that? You did this!'

'*Me?*' Damon's incredulous expression was a dead ringer for Cassie's. 'You think I've got nothing better to do with my time than play with other people's clothes? I didn't touch your stupid suitcase!'

Cassie pushed past Joel to go nose to nose with Damon in the corridor. 'If it wasn't you, then it was your idiot brother. But don't think I don't know that you're the brains behind it. If you can call it brains.'

'It wasn't me, it wasn't Tim, and it *definitely* wasn't

our dad,' he snapped right back at her. Damon was a good ten centimetres taller, but Cassie stood half on tiptoes to glare him in the eye. 'It wasn't any of us, psycho-girl!'

'Oh, you're trying to tell me *Joel* did it?' she said sarcastically.

Damon gave an obnoxious shrug. 'For all I know, you did it yourself. Trying to get us in trouble, *like always.*'

'You lot? In trouble? You get away with murder, and I get the blame for everything.'

Joel privately thought that Cassie usually got the blame because she started it, but he decided to keep that observation to himself. His sister looked about four seconds away from throwing punches, and he knew from experience that she knew how to do it too.

'What's going *on* up here?' Their mother came blazing up the stairs with a fury that was the twin of Cassie's. Tim appeared behind her, looking nervous, but wisely decided to hang back. Joel rather wished he could be over there out of the firing line with him.

Damon actually stepped back a few paces, looking intimidated, but Cassie just turned and flung an arm towards her ransacked bedroom. 'Mum! Look what they did to my room!'

Their mother looked at the room, then stepped back and stared up at the ceiling. Joel knew she was counting, the way she always did to calm herself down before she had a go at them.

In his experience, it rarely worked.

They all waited in agitated silence until she finally lowered her gaze to the three of them. She looked *extremely* annoyed, but when she spoke her voice was under tight control. 'OK,' she said softly. 'I don't care who did it— Quiet, Cassie! I don't care who started it. It stops, and it stops *now*, OK? No more fighting. Any of you.' Even Damon nodded solemnly.

'And now,' she said quietly, 'I am going to unpack. And I really don't want to come running up here again because you two are screaming at each other. Clear?'

'Clear,' said Damon quickly. Cassie nodded and looked at the floor, but Joel could see from where he stood that her expression was still sullenly angry.

As their mum left and the other boys rapidly departed, Joel lurked in the doorway uncertainly. 'Want some help?' he offered, as Cassie stood and looked at the state of her room.

'No,' she said brusquely. She kicked the corner of the folding bed so that it wobbled, and spun round. 'I'm going outside.'

Joel trailed behind her to the back door and out into the garden. It was spitting faintly, but Cassie didn't seem to care about the rain on her bare arms. She walked down to the bottom of the garden and stood looking up at the purple-grey sky. Joel stood silent beside her, hands stuck in the pockets of his jeans.

'I hate this place,' Cassie announced after several minutes. 'I hate *them*! We haven't been here five minutes and already Mum's taking their side over everything. It's always the same – right from the moment she met him everything's all about *Gerry*, and what perfect kids he's got, like they're the only ones that count any more and we're the ones getting in the way.'

'Maybe it won't be so bad,' Joel offered feebly. It

would have been more convincing if their new 'brothers' hadn't decided to give them a warm welcome by tossing Cassie's stuff around. If it *had* been them. Damon had sounded genuinely affronted to be accused, and he couldn't imagine it had been mild, nervous little Tim – but surely Cassie wouldn't make such a pointless attempt to frame them?

Cassie was in no mood to be reassured by her brother. She kicked at the dirt with the toe of one battered trainer. 'I can't believe this. I just can't believe this. What did we ever do to deserve *them*?'

'They're not all bad.' Joel struggled to defend them. 'What about Tim? Tim's OK.'

Cassie just pulled a face. 'Whatever,' she sighed. 'I don't care. I just don't want them here. I don't want to be here. I never did.'

There wasn't much to say to that, so the two of them just continued to stand there. The rain started to worsen, pelting down in icy droplets. The sky was overcast, turning the evening dark.

'Uh, getting wet now, Cass,' Joel observed. The rain was soaking into the cotton of his T-shirt, making it stick to him.

'You've always been wet,' she told him, but it was an automatic retort; there was no real bite in it. She just sounded tired, and depressed. 'Come on, then, Drippy. Back to the hell-house.'

They were moving back towards the back door when a bolt of lightning startled the life out of Joel. He was turning as it happened, and a flicker of movement caught the corner of his eye. He gripped his sister's arm urgently. 'Cassie, did you see that?'

'OK, that would be this stuff that we call lightning—'

'Over there!' A running figure, too slim and slight to be Damon, and entirely the wrong build for Tim. He was haring away as though he thought someone was after him.

'I didn't see anything.' Cassie turned round wildly. 'What? Over where?'

'There's someone in the garden.' He ran towards where he thought the lightning had highlighted the intruder. 'Hey! Hey!' Joel glimpsed the boy's face in another flare as he bolted hell for leather down the garden; it was contorted into a grimace of effort, and rendered deathly pale by more than just the poor visibility. He looked absolutely terrified. 'Hey, wait!' Joel yelled again.

The boy should have run straight into him for sure, or at least passed close enough to grab, but in the instant of blindness after the flash, Joel had somehow lost him.

'*Hey!* Wait up, what are you—? *Oof.*' He got caught up in a tangle of long grass and went sprawling. 'Ow.' He pushed himself up. 'Where the hell did he go?'

'Where did *who* go?' Cassie hovered over him, looking rather confused. 'Joel, I didn't see anybody.'

'Some kid.' He rubbed his elbow and looked around, but couldn't see anything through the driving rain. 'He must have come round the side of the house.' He glanced that way, and saw that the gate was locked and bolted. 'Or . . . from somewhere.' The side hedges were too high and too thick for anyone to have come through or over. The fence at the bottom was climbable, maybe, but that was the way the boy had been going, not coming from.

'Was it that idiot Damon?' Cassie asked with a scowl.

He shook his head. 'Too small. And it wasn't Tim,

either.' Joel hadn't made out much detail of the boy's features, but he'd seen the look on his face, and he didn't think he was going to forget it any time soon.

His sister shrugged dismissively. 'Probably some local kid on a dare, then. He might not have known that anyone's moved in yet.'

Joel glanced up at the house. He had to admit that in this kind of weather, it looked pretty imposing. What was sad and rather shabby in daylight was creepy as hell on a stormy night. 'You think this place is supposed to be haunted?'

He wanted to grasp onto that as a nice neat explanation, but somehow it was even more chilling than leaving the mystery unsolved. What kind of stories would people need to tell about this place for the kid to be *that* terrified? And, more to the point, what dark and terrible history might be behind them?

'Hey, maybe he just found out the Wilders have moved in. That's enough to frighten anybody.' Cassie shook her head. 'Come on, J, whoever he was he's gone now. I'm getting drenched.'

They made their way back inside, and the musty

smell seemed stronger than ever after the freshness of the rain. Cassie locked and bolted the door behind them.

'What're you doing that for?' Joel wondered, yanking his shoes off before he trod more mud all over the floor tiles. It was silly to feel guilty about making a mess considering the state of the house, but he still felt like a guest instead of a resident.

'Just in case it *was* that idiot Damon. If he's out in this, he can stay there.' She smiled grimly to herself.

But Joel knew it hadn't been either of the Wilders that he'd seen, and now that he'd had time to think, he was less and less sure that one of the village kids could even have got past them. The only way the boy could have got in was over the fence, and that was right where they'd been standing. He couldn't even have come through the house, since the front door still didn't open, so that only left the possibility of him hiding in the garden somewhere – and who would do that, in the middle of a thunderstorm?

And never mind where he'd come from, where had he *gone*? He'd somehow vanished completely at the very moment when he should have been within arm's reach. Joel stood by the kitchen window, squinting into the driving rain.

It was weird, very weird – and more than that, it was creepy. Who was that kid? How had he managed to come and go without being spotted? And, most important of all, what was he so afraid of?

J oel wriggled around in bed, trying to get more comfortable. Despite the cup of hot chocolate Cassie had made for him, he still felt chilled after the soaking he'd got falling face-first into wet grass. He hadn't even been able to have a warm shower like he would at home: there was only the bathtub, and he'd felt so creeped out and exposed taking a bath in that big, cold, dimly lit old room that he hadn't stayed in long. He kept getting the feeling someone was whispering to him every time he put his head underwater.

The bedroom was bothering him a little too, now that it was dark outside. His old room back home might have been pretty cramped, but at the same time it was snug. This one felt far too empty, and extremely cold. The huge window he'd been so delighted by rattled in its frame with every gust of wind. He was used to living with noises from the other flats, but this house made all sorts of alien creaks and groans, and he kept imagining he could hear people moving in the loft above his head.

The mystery of the boy in the garden continued to frustrate him. Joel knew he couldn't possibly come up with any more answers than he had already, and yet he couldn't seem to stop chewing it over in his mind.

However, it had been a long day, and Joel was very tired. Despite his churning thoughts, eventually he slipped into the clutches of a deep sleep, and troubled dreams.

He was running; running as fast as he possibly could, with his heart thundering in his chest and a sick taste in his mouth. He was fleeing through the rooms and corridors of the house – this house, he knew, though in his dream it seemed much bigger. It went on and on for ever, but that didn't mean he could keep running for ever, because his pursuer was gaining on him.

He pounded through the rooms with hammering footsteps and heavy, ragged breathing on his tail. And yet this wasn't some slavering monster; there was a little voice at the back of his mind telling him urgently that this was somebody he *knew*, somebody he trusted, and yet they were trying to kill him—

Joel jerked awake and upright in one motion, sucking in a great gasp of air. For a moment he was completely lost, the room a large, alien place where nothing was where it should be. Then reality kicked in, and he let out his breath in a long, shaky burst. He ran a hand through his hair, feeling the sweat that had pooled at the base of his neck.

In the dark he padded over to the big window and ducked behind the heavy curtains to stand in front of it. It took some fumbling and a quick thump to get it open, but the sudden blast of cool air was more than worth it. He just stood and breathed for a moment, taking in the fresh earthy smell of recent rain and trying to slow his rapidly beating heart.

There was someone standing at the bottom of the garden.

His heart skipped a beat entirely, and the breath caught in his throat and turned to ice. He saw it quite clearly, a pallid, upturned face peering towards his window – and then there was some minor shift in the clouds or the pattern of tree branches, and the image was gone. Joel clutched the corner of the window ledge.

Just an optical illusion. He forced himself to breathe. He needed to calm down, before he went completely crazy. It was only the last tatters of the disappearing nightmare intruding on his waking thoughts and painting the image of a face in moon-light reflected off . . . well, he couldn't figure out quite what. But it was surely only that. A chance pattern of light and shade, not really a face, not really somebody standing there.

He stood and stared out over the silent garden for a long time before returning to his bed.

When Joel woke again, to bright sunlight spilling through the curtains that he'd left slightly open, it was hard to remember the grip his night terrors had held over him. He entirely dismissed the idea of having seen a face. No doubt he had the stress of being stuck in the middle of Cassie and the Wilders to thank for his unusually vivid nightmares.

He dressed, and peeked round the door of Cassie's room to see what she was up to. She was lounging on the bed, reading one of her big history books. Cassie had a mad passion for history; she was always reading dry, boring books full of pictures of long-dead kings and queens. Joel had thought she would love staying in a house with a bit of a past, but of course the way things were she would never admit it even if she did.

Deciding not to disturb her, he made his way down to the kitchen, and found his mother and Gerald fiddling about with cloths and buckets and tools. 'What's going on?' he asked curiously, going through all the unfamiliar kitchen cupboards in search of cereal.

'Top left,' his mother advised him. She waved a metal scraper. 'We're making a start on some of the downstairs rooms, stripping all the old wallpaper off.'

'Cool. Can I help?' Joel figured that if Cassie was going to be difficult, it was up to him to try and build bridges around here. Besides, he didn't mind helping with the decorating. He and Cassie had always pitched in when their mother was trying to do anything in the flat, although she claimed they got in the way more than they helped.

Today, though, she rewarded him with a beam. 'Thank you, Joel. That would be lovely. But put your old clothes on first.' Gerald smiled at him too, and gave him a quick nod. Joel felt a bit sorry for Gerald. It wasn't as if he'd really *done* anything to make Cassie hate him so much.

Damon came down while he was still eating breakfast, fluffy haired and dishevelled. He flipped the kettle on and reached over Joel's head for the milk.

'You look tired,' Joel observed, looking for something to say. Somehow having people around at breakfast was twice as awkward and invasive as at any other time.

'Yeah.' Damon yawned into his hand. 'God, I was up at five o'clock this morning. I'm surprised Tim didn't wake you with the screaming. Some psychopath or something was trying to murder him in his dream, and when I woke him he thought that the guy had caught up with him. I tell you, I don't know *why* Dad lets him watch horror movies.' He shook his head, and flipped a tea bag into his mug.

Joel almost mentioned his own nightmare, but Tim was eighteen months younger than he was, and he didn't want to seem a complete baby. Instead he said, 'Your dad's starting on the wallpaper today.'

'Yeah,' Damon agreed. 'I said I'd give him a hand with that. There's loads of it to take off before he can even get started on the walls, and Tim's not exactly much use.'

'I said I'd help,' Joel told him.

Damon rewarded him with a flicker of a smile. 'Thanks. You're all right, you are. Not like your sister.'

Despite himself, Joel felt stupidly pleased by the casual compliment.

The four of them spent most of the morning stripping mouldy old wallpaper off the walls in the downstairs rooms. It wasn't particularly hard work, though the paper was pretty disgusting. They soaked it with water to help it come off more easily, and when Tim poked his head in later, Damon threw a ball of soggy paper at him and he ran off squealing. Damon grinned at Joel.

'That'll teach him to get me up in the middle of the night.'

Joel had expected Damon to be as spiky and argumentative as he usually was, but to his surprise the older boy was playful and quite friendly. He joked around with Joel and his father and even Joel's mother, but not spitefully. It seemed it was only Cassie who brought out his sharper side.

'You don't like Cassie, do you?' Joel observed, lying on his stomach to peel wallpaper away above the skirting board.

Damon shrugged. 'No offence, but she's a little bit nuts, isn't she? She acts like we're the spawn of the devil or something.'

Joel thought that was a pretty accurate assessment, but he couldn't exactly say so. 'It's not really you,' he told Damon. 'She just doesn't like how we all get squashed together and have to pretend we're a family or something.'

Damon snorted. 'Like it's great for any of us? She

needs to get over herself, that's her problem. No offence, but I don't really want you guys here any more than you want to be here. But you are, and there's no point pretending Dad and Amanda are going to change their minds or anything. She's just got to grow up and deal with it.'

'Yeah.' Joel couldn't help thinking how weird it was to hear his mother called Amanda. He wondered for the first time if it felt just as odd to the Wilders to hear their dad called Gerald. It was hard to remember sometimes that the three of them were intruding on Tim and Damon's lives just as much as the Wilders were on theirs.

Strangely enough, the idea that they were all as ill at ease as each other made everything feel more comfortable. They lapsed into a fairly companionable silence, and Joel decided that Damon wasn't so bad, really.

They kept working up until lunch time, when Joel's mother emerged from the kitchen to see how far they'd progressed. 'You boys doing OK in here?' she asked.

'We're fine,' agreed Damon, scrunching a long strip of paper into a ball. 'Almost done.'

'Food's nearly ready,' she told them. 'Shove all that loose paper in a black sack and put it out the back, would you? It can go in the skip when it arrives.'

'All right.' Joel straightened up.

'Oh, and Joel? Could you have a look in the boxes in my room when you've washed your hands? I can't find the bread knife – I think I must have shoved it in with the bedroom stuff when we left.'

'Yeah, you go on, Joel, I've got the rest of this,' Damon assured him.

'Sure? Cheers.' Joel scrubbed his hands clean in the bathroom and headed for the master bedroom. Aside from the loft and the cellar, it was the only part of the house he hadn't been in yet. He still felt a little funny knowing that his mother was sharing it with Gerald.

It was a warm day, but the metal doorknob must have retained the cold, because he hissed in dismay when he grasped it. The door bounced open awkwardly as he released it too quickly in surprise.

The room was bigger than his own, of course, but with the double bed taking up most of the floor it didn't look nearly so bare. The brightly coloured modern furniture seemed out of place against the dark wooden floor and pale walls.

The contrast between the unfamiliar quilt with its pattern of red roses and his mother's bedside cabinet from home was somehow even more disconcerting. It would have been easier to walk into a room where everything was different than one where the new was mixed in with the old so obtrusively.

For a moment Joel tried to imagine how this room must once have looked, with old-fashioned wooden furniture and an elegant cream-coloured eiderdown. That picture seemed somehow truer, more permanent than the one before him now – and when he glanced back at the bed, the bright red flowers looked like bloodstains, marring a surface that should have been pale and clean.

He shook his head to clear it of the disturbing mental image, and hurried over to the boxes in the corner. This room was creeping him out, with its jarring combination of things that didn't quite belong together.

And why was it so *cold* in here? He'd been sweating all morning stripping off wallpaper, and now he was getting goosebumps. He looked in the closest of the unopened boxes, eager to be finished and get out of here.

There was a small click from behind him, and Joel jumped a mile. He called himself an idiot when he realized it was only the door. It must have been slowly swinging shut ever since it bounced off the wall when he opened it.

Except . . . hadn't he stopped it with his hand for exactly that reason? Joel sat very still on his haunches, clearly seeing himself doing it. He had, he definitely had . . .

'Hello?' he said aloud a little shakily, thinking perhaps one of the others had come up behind him and pushed the door closed in passing. Except that the door opened *inwards*, so that didn't really make any sense whatsoever . . .

Nobody answered.

He was obviously losing his marbles. Nonetheless, he would be a lot happier if he could be out of this room extremely quickly. He started scrabbling through the boxes carelessly, throwing things this way and that in his hurry to be done. Bread knife – where was the stupid bread knife? It ought to be on the top if it had been packed last thing . . . Ah.

Joel finally spotted the wooden handle down the side of one of the boxes, and squeezed his fingers in to prise it out. 'Come *on*, you— Thank you.' He got a proper grip on the handle and yanked it out. And found himself holding a long, sharp dagger, the blade thick with dripping blood.

He dropped it with a wordless cry, and it bounced across the floorboards. For a moment it lay in a spreading pool of blood . . . and then it was just a bread knife, completely clear of bloodstains and entirely the wrong shape to try and stab anybody with.

Joel stared at the knife. It didn't change. He wanted to get *out* of here, urgently, but he couldn't bring himself to pick it up.

Finally he shoved the door open and kicked the knife in the direction of the hallway, barely looking down in case he saw the trail of blood that his imagination expected it to leave. It bounced off the doorframe and out, and he scrambled hastily after it.

And the door, which this time he hadn't touched at all, slammed shut.

Joel was still feeling shaky when he sat down to lunch, although nobody seemed to notice. Cassie had brought her history book down with her, and spent the whole meal with her nose in that. Normally their mother would have told her off for reading at the table, but today she was probably just happy that his sister wasn't making a scene.

He still hadn't quite wrapped his head around what had happened to him in the bedroom. He could almost have explained it away as a momentary hallucination, if it hadn't been for the way the door had moved. Well, the house was in quite a state, and perhaps things were warped out of shape or badly balanced or . . . something. And he was clearly overtired.

Seriously overtired.

He accepted Tim's rather shy invitation to play chess after lunch, despite the fact that he was pretty bad at the game. Anything to take his mind off the utter strangeness of what had just happened to him with that knife.

They set up the board on the dining table, since there wasn't much furniture anywhere else yet. 'Black or white?' Tim asked, holding out a pair of pawns from his rather nice carved chess set.

'Either. Trust me, I can lose in record time whatever colour I'm playing.'

Joel quite liked spending time with Tim. He was a quiet, rather anxious boy, not much like his father or brother at all. He smiled a lot, but never said much, and he always cringed when Cassie and Damon were arguing. Joel was sure he was pretty smart, but he obviously didn't like being the centre of attention.

He was certainly good at chess. Joel never had

quite enough patience for strategy games at the best of times, and today he was missing even more obvious threats than usual. 'You're too good at this,' he grumbled cheerfully, as they got to checkmate for the second time after far too short a game.

Tim actually blushed. 'We can do something else, if you want.'

He shrugged. 'No, it's OK. I'll get you this time.' The only other person he usually played was Cassie, so he was used to getting stomped. 'You should play my sister,' he suggested, as they began setting up the board again. 'She's pretty good, but you might still beat her. You really are good at it.'

Tim looked worried. 'Your sister's scary,' he confessed in a low voice.

Joel laughed. 'Yeah. She is a bit,' he agreed with a grin. 'She'll get used to you, though.' He hoped.

'Hey, kids. Having fun?' His mother stopped to give them both a smile on her way through the room.

He nodded. 'Tim's completely thrashing me at chess.'

'You should castle,' his mother advised. 'Protect your king.'

Joel raised his eyebrows. 'You didn't even look at the board.'

'Well, it's the only chess move I actually know the name for.' She headed into the kitchen. 'Now, do either of you boys remember what crazy thing I decided to do with the biscuits when we unpacked? I'd just about kill for a cup of tea and a—' She stopped dead.

'Mum?' Joel worriedly scrambled to his feet.

She emerged with a stormy look on her face, and ignored him to walk out into the hall and call upstairs. 'Cassandra Demetrius! Here. *Now.*' Tim and Joel exchanged nervous looks.

Cassie came thundering down the stairs, looking unsure whether she should be annoyed or nervous. 'Hey! What did I—?'

'Come with me.' Their mother grabbed her by the shoulder and marched her into the kitchen and over to the back door. The two boys followed, and gasped at what they saw.

The neatly tied rubbish sacks that Damon had left on the back step earlier were no longer there. Instead, they and their contents were strewn all over the huge garden. It looked as if someone had hacked them to pieces with a knife, and then kicked and thrown all the scraps of old wallpaper as far away as possible. There was wallpaper and black plastic wrapped round tree trunks and caught up in branches *everywhere*.

Joel's jaw dropped. Surely Cassie wouldn't have done something like this – would she?

For a moment his mind flew back to the hallucination he'd had in the master bedroom. That sharp, deadly blade, completely unlike the bread knife it should have been . . . Perfect, in fact, for slicing things to ribbons.

Which was nuts, of course. Nobody was going around stabbing anything with imaginary knives. There had to be a more mundane culprit, senseless as the whole thing seemed.

Their mother certainly seemed to think Cassie was to blame. 'Suppose you explain this to me, young lady?' she said icily.

His sister's eyes were alight with fiery disbelief. 'I— It *wasn't me!*' she insisted. And to Joel's ears, it sounded like she was telling the truth.

But maybe it was only to his own ears, because

their mother's expression didn't change. 'If you didn't do it, who did?'

'Damon!' she insisted quickly. '*Him!*' She pointed at Tim, who shrank back looking dismayed. 'Not *me*!'

Joel saw his mother's eyes narrow. 'You think they'd *deliberately* and maliciously mess up all their father's hard work?'

'If it got *me* in trouble!' Cassie insisted. 'My room—'

'I'm beginning to wonder if you didn't do that yourself,' she cut her off sharply. 'I've had quite enough of you, young lady. I don't know what makes you think you can get away with stunts like this; Lord knows I raised you better than that. Well, there'll be no more. You're going to clean up every scrap of that paper *right now*. And then you're going to apologize to Gerald. I'm not having this. I'm just not.'

'I *didn't do it!*' Cassie sounded close to frustrated tears now.

Gerald had appeared in the doorway behind them. 'OK, OK,' he said, holding up his hands and looking alarmed. 'Everybody just calm down. Amanda, it's not such a big deal. We can easily—'

Joel's mother refused to be placated. 'Oh, no. Enough is enough. Gerald, I've been putting up with this for entirely too long.' She turned back to Cassie. 'Cassandra, it's about time you learned there are *consequences* to your actions. You're not a two-year-old, and I don't expect this kind of behaviour from you.'

Cassie had given up protesting, and shrugged sullenly. 'You're not going to believe me whatever I say, so why should I bother? OK, I'll clean your stupid garden up. But I'm not apologizing, because I *didn't do it*.' She stormed out.

Gerald reached out to their mother, who leaned up against him gratefully and sighed. 'I'm sorry, Gerry, really. I don't know what's got into the girl.'

Gerald smiled at her. 'It's OK. It's probably her age. This isn't easy on any of the kids, and she's the only girl here. Two extra brothers is enough to give anybody a headache. She'll get over it.'

'I hope,' she agreed with a sigh.

'Come on. Let's go back inside.' The two adults moved off together, and Tim and Joel were left to give each other troubled glances.

'You think she did it?' asked Tim nervously.

Joel could only shrug. 'I don't know,' he admitted. He would have liked to say no . . . but who else could it have been? This time he was certain it hadn't been Damon. The two of them had spent the whole morning getting this stuff off the walls, and why would Damon want to mess up something he and his father had been working so hard on?

For a moment he thought of the boy he'd seen the previous night. Could it have been him? But why? Just for the sake of causing trouble?

Maybe it was irrational, but he was sure that the boy he'd seen running through the garden had not had any thought of vandalism on his mind. He'd looked like the only thing he could begin to care about was getting away from the house as fast as possible. Joel couldn't imagine anybody who'd been that terrified returning to the scene of their fright voluntarily.

He peered outside to where a forlorn-looking Cassie was angrily yanking paper out of one of the trees. Whether she'd done it herself or not, she was still his sister. I'm going to help her, he decided.

He waded through the long grass to join Cassie. 'Oh,' she said flatly. 'It's you.' She pulled on a scrap of wallpaper so hard the twigs catching it snapped.

'I'll help,' he offered, kneeling down to start gathering more of the paper.

'Why not?' She shrugged. 'They're already punishing *me* when I didn't do anything – you might as well get in on the act.'

'Um . . .' They both turned to see Tim lurking awkwardly behind them. 'I could help, if you like . . .'

'No, you couldn't.' Cassie scowled. 'Why don't you get back in your house with your brain-dead brother? We don't want *you* following us around.'

Tim hesitated, looking dismayed, but then backed away towards the house. Cassie just turned her back on him, but Joel gave a pantomime shrug and mouthed 'Sorry' helplessly. When the other boy was gone, he elbowed his sister in the side.

'Give it a rest, Cass! He was only trying to help.'

'I don't *want* his help,' Cassie said fiercely. 'They're all as bad as each other. Well, fine. They don't want me here, and I don't want to *be* here. I'm going to leave. Just walk right out of this garden, and keep on walking.'

Joel raised his eyebrows at her, trying to work out

if she was serious. He didn't think so, but it was pretty hard to tell. 'You can't,' he said. 'You don't even know this place.' The old house was on the edge of a little village, right in the middle of nowhere. 'Where would you go?'

'Anywhere that isn't here,' she muttered. 'I might as well; Mum wouldn't even miss me.'

'Of course she would,' insisted Joel, injured. 'Cass, you know she's not really picking on you. She just really wants this to work.' And Cassie really wanted to mess it up for her. Why did she *think* it wasn't going down well?

'Yeah, well, she's not even giving me the benefit of the doubt, is she?' She kicked the nearest tree. 'You heard her. *Gerald's* kids get the benefit of the doubt, but not us. She didn't even think for a minute that it might not have been me.'

'Well, you *have* been the one doing all the fighting . . .' Joel defended their mother weakly.

Cassie turned on him, fiery-eyed. 'Oh, you as well, is it? You think I did this?'

'No!' he replied automatically, although he still wasn't totally sure.

She inspected his expression for a moment, then sighed and relaxed a little. 'Yeah. You know why? Because you're my little brother, and you trust me. Unlike *others* in this house I could mention.'

'Yeah.' Joel shrugged uncomfortably, and changed the subject. 'Come on, Cass. Let's go and get some more sacks to put this in or something. It won't take that long to collect the rest of it up.'

His sister might have a hot temper, but she was hardly one for senseless vandalism. It was difficult to believe this could have been her work – but he had to admit she was the most likely suspect. Maybe Gerald was right about this whole thing being stressful for her.

However, as he hauled himself halfway up a tree to unwind a shredded length of black plastic that had caught there, Joel began to wonder . . . Exactly how was his sister supposed to have hacked up all these rubbish sacks without messing up her clothes, and without any of them hearing her sneak back in afterwards?

They spent the rest of the afternoon gathering up scraps of wallpaper and plastic from the garden; some of them had probably flown away over the village by now, but that was somebody else's problem.

Joel did his best to try and cheer up Cassie and stop her brooding, but it didn't work. None of his usual clowning around produced a smile, and when he offered to finish the punishment for her, she refused.

'Oh, no,' she said dangerously, shaking her head. 'Wouldn't want people to think I *didn't do what I was told*, now would we?'

He was pretty sure Cassie wouldn't take this latest incident lying down. Whether she was behind it or not, she was clearly furious that her mother had automatically assumed she was to blame. With a pair of hot tempers like Cassie's and Damon's involved, he shuddered to think how quickly things might escalate.

To his relief, however, his sister seemed to have settled on sulking rather than going for immediate revenge. When they were finally finished and cleaned up, Cassie retreated to her bedroom and her books and wouldn't come out. She didn't even emerge when Gerald called up the stairs, 'Hey, kids, come and have a look at this!'

Joel and the other boys ran downstairs to join him in the kitchen.

'I finally managed to open up the cellar,' he revealed with a slight smile. 'Hey, Damon, you'll never guess why I couldn't get it open before.'

'Why?'

'You know those nails in the door that I thought were a clumsy repair job?'

'It was actually nailed shut?' Damon asked incredulously.

'Yup. Mad, I know. But it just goes to show that you shouldn't underestimate the insane things people will do in the name of DIY. There was probably a cabinet in front of the door before, or they just didn't like the draught – who knows?'

Joel took a peek down the steps into the darkness below and wrinkled his nose. 'God, it stinks down there.'

'Well, I've got no idea how long it's been shut up. At least twelve years – that's how long it's been since the last owners left, and apparently they weren't here for very long. The house has been empty most of the time since it was built. Nobody seems to have wanted to stick around – maybe they were daunted by the size of the repair job this place needs.'

'Maybe,' said Joel. And for some reason found himself thinking of a bloody knife on the floor of the master bedroom.

Gerald clapped his hands. 'But anyway, here's the interesting bit. While I was rooting around down there, I found this.' He indicated a rather battered-looking cardboard box in the corner of the kitchen. 'I'm not sure what it is – looks like a lot of paperwork and old photos – but it's been down there for some time. It's the kind of thing I thought your sister might be interested in,' he said to Joel, sounding rather hopeful.

'Maybe,' he agreed noncommittally, knowing that she probably would be but she'd die before she admitted it to Gerald.

'All right. Well, anyway, I wouldn't advise you to start scrabbling through that stuff now – your dinner's nearly ready. You should probably go and call your sister down, Joel.'

'OK.'

He did, but Cassie refused point blank to come down to dinner. Gerald looked troubled, but their mother just shrugged. 'Let her stay up there,' she decided. 'She's become a right little madam lately, and I don't like it one bit. If she gets hungry, that's her problem. She has to learn that these kinds of tricks won't work on me any more.'

Joel just bent over his dinner, not meeting anyone's eye, and vowed to sneak up sandwiches or something for her later.

However, after the meal he got dragged into

playing another game of chess with Gerald, and Tim and Damon started watching a movie that he stayed to see the end of. When the grown-ups took over the TV-watching he intended to go and check on Cassie, but Damon cornered him first. 'You want to come check out the loft with us?' he asked. 'We're going to go up there with a torch. It'll be cool.'

Joel shifted uncomfortably. 'Cassie . . .' he began.

'Oh, let her rot in there.' Damon shrugged. 'She brought it on herself. Psycho-girl.'

'What if she really didn't do it?' Joel tried to suggest.

Damon rolled his eyes. 'Come on, man, wake up and smell the coffee. I know she's your sister, but if she didn't do it, who did? It wasn't you, it wasn't us, and it sure as hell wasn't your mum.'

'I suppose,' he had to agree reluctantly.

'Exactly. So, are you coming with us or what?'

'OK,' he agreed. Cassie probably wouldn't have talked to him anyway, and it wasn't like he had anything better to do. Despite himself, he felt a flash of resentment towards his older sister. Why should things have to be hellish for him here just because *she* was unhappy?

True to his word, Damon dug the torch out of his father's tool kit, and they crept back through the house by torchlight. 'Why don't we just turn the lights on?' Tim asked uneasily.

'Because it's cooler this way,' said Damon. 'Come on.' He led them through the front hall and up the stairs.

It was funny how, even though they'd gone back and forth across this landing all day, it looked so completely different in darkness. They might have moved in, but the house still felt like it was empty, and Joel felt a nervous tightness across his belly despite himself.

It was stupid. They were just big old rooms – he'd been through the whole house yesterday. He knew that, but his nerves remained on edge, the house still too unfamiliar to feel quite safe.

They all jumped as Damon abruptly clicked off the torch, and Tim let out a little squeak of fright. 'Damon!' he said indignantly.

His brother switched the torch on again just long enough to light up his smirk. 'What's up, kids? Afraid of the dark?'

'You're doing my eyes in, man,' Joel objected as he switched it off again. He would die before he admitted it, but the dark *was* bothering him. He kept thinking of that dream where he'd been running through the rooms of this house, being chased.

And it was just that – a dream. Why was he obsessing over it?

As his eyes readjusted, he realized that the only light he could see was a thin band at floor level, spilling out from under a door. 'Must be coming from Cassie's room,' he said, nudging Tim.

'We should wait for her to come out and then jump out and scare the hell out of her,' suggested Damon wickedly.

'Oh, *don't*,' pleaded Joel uneasily. The last thing he needed was Cassie getting the idea he was on the Wilders' side.

'Oh, come on,' grinned Damon. 'It'd be funny!'

'No it wouldn't. She'd totally explode. Besides, she's in one of her sulks. She might not come out for hours.'

'Yeah. OK.' Damon led the way quietly past Cassie's room. Joel knew that the room right next to it was his – and yet, that didn't seem to make the gaping doorway any less ominous.

'Put the torch back on, Damon,' begged Tim nervously.

His brother clapped him on the shoulder. 'Oh, don't wuss out on me now, Timmy. Joel's not scared, are you, Joel?'

'No,' he lied immediately. 'It's just a house.' It was easy to tell them that – much harder to convince himself. In his mind's eye he saw the bloody knife, and imagined somebody creeping through the darkness behind them . . .

'Yeah. Just a house.' Damon shrugged. 'Come on. Up here.' He had to stretch to snag the pull handle and bring the hatch door down. The ladder slithered down after it with a series of scrapes and clangs that made Joel wince.

He followed Damon gingerly up the rickety ladder, placing his feet cautiously in the darkness. The rungs had a nasty gritty, greasy feel to them; he shuddered to think what the palms of his hands would look like when he could see them again. How long had it been since anyone was last up here?

Joel reached the top and scrambled away from the hatch, coughing in the stirred-up dust. He stayed kneeling, unsure of the height to the ceiling. The shapeless darkness was unnerving; was there room for someone else to be hiding up there? Someone sitting silently in the dark and waiting for an unsuspecting visitor to climb up and pull the hatch closed behind them . . .

He remembered the faint sounds in the night that had seemed so much like footsteps up above, and swallowed.

Tim came up last, more tentatively even than Joel. 'This floor doesn't sound safe,' he observed uneasily.

'Course it's safe, Tim, you're not as fat as all that.' Damon's voice echoed oddly in the darkness, and Joel heard the floor creak as he shifted position. Just like he had done the night before . . . 'Besides, Dad's already been up here. If he didn't fall through the floor, none of us are going to. Come on, close the hatch.'

As Tim reluctantly pulled the ladder up and shut them in, Joel was suddenly hyper-aware of how enclosed they were. He knew that the air couldn't possibly change that fast, but all the same his chest immediately felt tighter.

'I don't like this,' Tim whispered solemnly, close to his ear.

Joel said nothing, but inside his head he had to agree. This was creepy. 'Damon, where are you?' he asked quietly. There was no reason why they shouldn't talk just as loudly as they liked – it wasn't late, not the midnight it felt like – but something about the dark made him want to be quiet. Just in case there might be something out there, listening . . .

'Here.' Damon's voice was just as subdued, coming from somewhere to the side. 'There's a door over here – come and check it out.'

Joel stumbled blindly towards him. Tim grabbed hold of his wrist so as not to lose him, and he couldn't say he minded very much.

He almost bit his tongue in shock when he walked into a warm shape in the darkness. Damon, of course – who else? He was completely losing it. 'Just use the torch, Damon, this is stupid,' he advised.

'Yeah.' Was it his imagination, or did Damon sound just a little anxious himself? A moment later the circle of light sprang back to life, seeming very feeble and insignificant.

Joel eyed the door, unreasonably troubled by it. This house had hidden corners, secrets. There was a subtle but pervasive feeling of things being not quite right that hung over everything.

'Why are we doing this?' he asked with a kind of slight chuckle, because it was easier to sound as if he was a little bored than admit he was getting creeped out.

''Cos there's nothing better to do.' Damon grabbed the door handle and yanked. 'Here we go. Through here.'

He held the door open, and Tim reluctantly shuffled through it. He came to an abrupt halt. 'Hey! This is a cupboard.'

'Is it?' With a grin, Damon quickly slammed the door behind him.

'Damon!' Tim sounded genuinely panicked as he tried to push back from inside. 'Damon, let me out!' He thumped on the inside of the door with increasing urgency.

His brother was still tightly gripping the doorknob,

and Joel nudged him in the side, alarmed. 'Damon! It's not *funny*. Let him out!'

The older boy turned towards him, and even in the torchlight Joel saw the rising panic in his eyes. 'I'm *trying* to! It's stuck!'

'It's OK, Tim!' Damon yelled through the door. 'It's OK! I'm trying to get you out! Don't panic.' If anything, the thumping from the inside of the cupboard grew even more urgent.

Damon hauled ineffectually on the handle again, and Joel elbowed him aside. 'Let me try.' The handle didn't twist, and neither straight-out tugging nor attempting to jiggle it worked. The door was stuck as firmly as if it were bolted in place. 'Did it lock?' he asked Damon nervously.

'It couldn't have done.' The older boy looked deeply worried; he obviously hadn't planned for his little prank to go this far. 'I should get Dad.'

'Damon!' The muffled yell from inside sounded even more panicked. 'Get me out!'

'Don't go, Damon, he'll totally freak out,' Joel advised him nervously.

Damon shot him an incredulous look. 'He's *already* freaked out. Tim!' He raised his voice. 'Tim, Tim, can you hear me? I need you to hit the door where it's stuck. Over here where the handle is on this side.'

'Will that help?' asked Joel worriedly.

Damon could only shrug. 'I don't know!' He resumed tugging on the door handle. 'Come on, Tim, help me out here!' He kicked the bottom corner of the door, and yanked with all his might. Joel could actually see the muscles moving in his arms; how could the door remain jammed?

Tim suddenly yelped, and there was a flurry of thumps from inside the cupboard. Joel wasn't sure whether he was following instructions or just wildly battering at the walls in a blind panic. 'Let me *out*!' His voice rose into a panicked screech that could have belonged to a child about eight years younger.

'I'm trying, Timmy, I swear!' Damon was beginning to sound as distressed as his brother.

Tim didn't even seem to be hearing them. 'Just let me go! Please, just let me *out*!' he pleaded desperately, as if they were keeping him prisoner instead of fighting with all their might to get him out.

Joel made a decision. 'I'm getting your dad,' he told Damon, and sprinted for the hatch. He was only halfway to it when Damon gave a sudden grunt of surprise and the door flew open. Tim stumbled out, on his way to collapsing if his brother hadn't caught him.

'Tim!' Joel dashed back over, seeing how pale he looked as Damon shone the torch on him. 'Hey, you all right?'

Damon gave his little brother a squeeze and ruffled his hair. 'I'm sorry, Timmy, I'm sorry,' he said, sounding sincere. 'I didn't mean it. Jeez, I'm sorry.'

'I'm OK,' insisted Tim weakly, not really looking it. He looked more like he was about to throw up.

'Sorry,' Damon repeated. 'Stupid door must have stuck.'

'Let me have a look,' Joel requested, taking the

torch when Damon offered it to him. He played the light over the doorway: there was quite clearly no lock, nor even a catch or a magnet. It was just a simple lightweight cupboard door that was supposed to open with a touch. 'The wood must have warped or something. There's nothing I can see to hold it.'

'It was fine when I was up here with Dad the other day, I swear,' Damon said.

Joel gave him a look. 'You knew it was a cupboard? And you shut him in it? I can't believe you just did that!'

'It was a joke, OK!' he said, shrugging defensively. 'I couldn't resist it – you two were both looking so freaked out. How was I supposed to know it was going to stick? What am I, psychic?'

'I'm OK,' Tim repeated, but he sounded rather subdued.

'All right, then. Sorry, Tim. Give us the torch back, Joel.'

Joel was still more than a little freaked out, though he'd die before he admitted it, and he would have gladly got out of there if something hadn't caught his eye.

'Wait a second, I just want to look at something.'

The torchlight had picked out some marks low down on the inside wall, piquing his curiosity. 'Don't let that door slam again,' he added as an afterthought, as he was about to step inside.

'I've got it,' Damon assured him.

Joel stepped inside the cupboard and knelt down for a closer look. Somebody had scratched, in a child's round, laborious handwriting, '*Michael H.*'. The carving looked extremely old. He grinned, reaching out to touch the old graffiti. 'Huh. Looks like somebody—'

It was not a sound or a movement that cut off his words, but a sudden sensation; a lurch of his stomach like the start of a rollercoaster, and a chill so complete that his breath puffed out in a visible cloud. He gasped in shock as something that felt like a small, cold hand grabbed hold of his leg.

Whispers were crowding through his brain, below the level of hearing but human enough and urgent enough to make choking panic rise up in his throat. All the air had bled out of the room and from his lungs. The grip on his leg tightened to vice-like proportions, but he couldn't make himself look down, or even move.

Joel heard a door open somewhere far below. The

noise was too faint, a phantom breath of a sound, and he didn't know if it was real or only in his head. There was a small whimper of fright that sounded far too loud in the darkness, and he wasn't sure if he was the one who had made it.

Then, abruptly, the pressure of those unseen fingers was gone. The paralysis fled with it, and he lunged for the cupboard door – jamming his shoulder into the gap just as it slammed.

Outside, Damon swore loudly. 'I didn't—'

'Help me!' Even with Joel's body trapped against it, the door refused to give. It took both Wilders hauling on the edge to move it, and Joel winced in pain as he fought his way out, struggling for every millimetre against a force that seemed stronger than gravity. As soon as he'd squeezed out, the cupboard door shut itself with a violent bang.

Damon stared at it, then turned back to Joel. 'What happened in there?'

He shook his head mutely and just breathed for a few seconds. 'Let's just – let's get out of this loft.'

'OK.' Damon didn't argue, and Tim was already fumbling to let down the ladder.

Joel was shaking as he scrambled down, convinced the folding ladder would snap closed to trap his hands or collapse under him. The light that Tim switched on as he left the bottom rung did nothing to settle him; it seemed too bright, unnatural, a false reassurance.

Damon jumped down after him, looking pale and sweaty. 'There must be . . . it has to be some kind of weird balance thing up there,' he said, pushing back his hair from his forehead. 'Maybe the walls have shifted or . . . something, and gravity keeps trying to pull it shut.'

His tone was not as casual as the words, and Joel noticed that his shoulders didn't relax until he'd pushed the ladder back up and secured the hatch. He turned round and ruffled Tim's hair again. 'You all right now, kid?'

'Yeah.' He smiled for his brother, but turned a look on Joel that seemed equal parts nervous and defensive. 'I wouldn't normally panic like that,' he said quickly.

'No.' Joel would have hastened to assure him he believed that, if he hadn't still been fighting to steady himself after his own brush with abject terror.

'It's just . . .' Tim breathed out slowly. 'For a moment there, I really thought . . . It really felt like I was trapped in there with somebody else.'

He moved off before Joel could think of anything to say.

Try as he might, Joel couldn't dismiss the experience up in the loft as easily as he had the momentary hallucination with the bread knife. He still shivered as he remembered that unseen hand taking hold of his leg. He hadn't just witnessed a brief optical illusion; he'd been held, grabbed, forced back by a door that had no one else touching it.

At least, no one visible.

Joel still hadn't shaken off the prickling feeling of discomfort by the time he was standing in the bathroom, getting ready for bed. He found himself staring at the rack of toothbrushes, pondering how strange it was to see six instead of three, and conscious of trying too hard to think about that and not about more disturbing things.

The bathroom and kitchen were the only rooms that still had any kind of fixtures and fittings – Joel supposed because it was easier to leave them than take them away. There was a big old mirror over the basin, the kind with one of those over-the-top gilt frames. His mother had laughed out loud when she first saw it. 'Not the most classy piece in the world,' she had pronounced.

Joel leaned over to spit toothpaste into the sink, and froze. Something had moved in the mirror; just a flash of motion, barely more than a shadow. Heart suddenly hammering in his chest again, he straightened up.

He stood eye to eye with his reflection for a long moment. The mirror had a slightly tarnished look, so that everything it reflected seemed duller than it really was. It made the room behind him look very dark, and some kind of bulge or distortion in the glass magnified it and twisted it out of shape.

A whisper of a noise behind him made his hair stand on end, and he whipped round. Nothing. Joel just stood there, holding perfectly still, while his pulse rushed in his ears and his breathing seemed to become unnaturally loud. He *knew* there was nothing there – and yet he couldn't bring himself to turn his back on the room again. Stronger even than the voice of logic was the gut certainty that the second he turned round, something would move.

He was conscious of a faint dripping from behind him, forming a slow and ominous counterpoint to his overactive heartbeat. Just the tap. He tried to will his taut nerves to stop twanging. He couldn't have turned it tightly enough, that was all. He reached backwards without turning . . . and his fingers touched something soft and warm.

Joel jumped a mile, and then realized it was only his flannel. Letting out a huff of self-mocking laughter and finally relaxing, he turned round to wring it out in the sink.

The water that trickled out of it was pale pink, and when he looked down, his hands were covered in blood.

VIII

Joel dropped the blood-soaked cloth with a cry of revulsion and jumped backwards. His own movement immediately drew his eye to the mirror, and for a fraction of a second he saw a pale face reflected there that was not his own.

Then it was gone, and he was just looking at himself, wide-eyed and cringing back against the bathroom wall.

The flannel lay on the floor where it had fallen, a perfectly innocuous faded blue, and soaked with nothing worse than soapy warm water. It was a while before he could bring himself to pick it up between finger and thumb and quickly fling it back into the corner.

When he'd sat down on the floor and breathed for long enough to convince himself he wasn't having a heart attack, Joel left the bathroom and went upstairs. The thought of his own empty bedroom was too daunting, and he dropped in on Cassie instead.

'Hey, Cass,' he said, striving hard not to sound too wobbly.

His sister was in her pyjamas, legs tucked up under her as she read her book. She hadn't been downstairs all evening, and if she was hungry, she wasn't admitting it.

'Hey, you,' she said flatly, not looking up. Joel padded across the cold floorboards and hopped up to sit on the bed beside her.

It was difficult to figure out exactly how to broach the subject; he wasn't even really sure what the subject *was*. Was there really something supernatural going on in this house, or was it all in his own head? Maybe he was going crazy. Tim seemed to feel it too – but then, Tim was easy spooked, and there was a world of difference between feeling creeped out and hallucinating knives and dripping blood all over the place.

'Listen, I've been – I've been looking around the house,' he tried.

'Yeah, with your new favourite siblings,' Cassie growled, turning a page. 'I heard.'

His sister's hostility suddenly seemed twice as petty and irritating as before. 'Listen, Cassie, they are *not* the problem, OK?'

'Oh, and I am, I suppose?'

'No.' He forced himself to calm down. He was too on edge to step around Cassie's temper as he did normally. 'Look, I've been thinking. About what happened this afternoon with the rubbish and everything – what if it wasn't the Wilders trying to stitch you up at all?'

Cassie lowered her book and gave him a dubious look. 'Exactly who else are we suspecting here? This mysterious fence-climbing local kid of yours?'

Joel was suddenly sure that the boy he'd seen the night before wasn't a trespasser from the village at all. 'Well . . . what if it wasn't actually a person?'

'Ah, the lawn mower went into attack mode. Yeah, I've heard that can happen.' She raised an eyebrow at him.

'Cassie . . .' He sighed. His sister would probably think he was nuts whatever he said; how was he supposed to know himself? Still, he had to try. 'Have you noticed anything, well, strange about this house?'

'Aside from the occupants?'

He gave her an unamused look. 'Yes.'

She shrugged. 'I don't know. What kind of strange?'

He found that he just couldn't bring himself to start babbling about blood and knives and invisible hands. 'Well, it's . . . there are all these hidden corners and boarded-up bits and nobody seems to want to live here. I was just thinking . . . I mean, doesn't it seem kind of creepy to you? Maybe there's something about the house that makes people—'

Cassie just laughed at his expression. 'Nobody wants to stay because it's a *dump*, Joel. You don't get a place like this cheap unless the people flogging it to you are worried bits are going to fall off. Mum says some rich weirdo designed and built the place himself back in the fifties. For all we know, he filled it with six thousand cats and nobody wanted to move in after he'd gone. It's no big mystery. A fancy custom-built house like this is going to be too expensive if it's in good nick, and too much work if it's not. Only a nutter like Gerald would think it was a good deal.'

'And Mum,' Joel pointed out.

'Yeah, well, she's the one who's marrying Gerald Wilder, so I don't think we can exactly vouch for her sanity.'

Joel knew the conversation was going to go downhill if they got into this again. And, try as he might, he couldn't think of a single way to explain what he'd been seeing and feeling since they arrived that wouldn't end with Cassie laughing out loud at him.

'Ghosts, Joel?' she'd say. 'You're losing your mind.' And he wasn't at all sure he could disagree.

And yet . . . Maybe he could have believed that it had all been in his head if he had only the blood-filled hallucinations to go on. But Tim had felt the presence up in the loft, and all of them had seen that door move and hold itself shut – and if he was right about Cassie's room and the rubbish sacks and that boy he thought he'd seen out in the garden . . .

Before switching the light off and getting into bed, Joel pulled up his pyjama leg and examined the tender skin beneath. A bruise was already beginning to form below his knee. It looked an awful lot like it had been left by fingers.

He took a long time to fall asleep that night, and when he did he fell into dark, tense dreams.

It was pitch black and the dark was pressing in all around him. He was squeezed down on his knees, crammed into a space that was almost too tight for him. Joel could feel the warmth of another body pressed up against him, a smaller boy shaking violently with terror. For a moment he thought it was Tim, but then he wasn't sure.

With a sudden flash of certainty, he knew where they were. They were up there in the loft, him and this other boy, crammed together in the cupboard because somebody, something, was prowling around outside. Looking for them.

His own breath rattled in his ears; so loud – too loud – that he almost wanted to strangle himself to cut it off. *Please don't let him find me,* he thought, without even truly knowing in his mind who 'he' might be. *Please, don't let him find me. Please, don't let him—*

The other boy's breath was a laboured hissing just

on the edge of hearing. For a moment Joel thought it was just frightened panting, but then he realized that hidden in that whispered breath were words, a chant as endless and senseless as the one inside his head.

He didn't really want to understand the words, but as soon as he knew they were there he seemed powerless to stop his brain from seeking them out, finding the sense in the rhythm of the chant that was hammering its way into his head. It was a chant he knew, a prayer, or part of one, but seeming suddenly horrible in the way it had been cut short.

'If I should die before I wake, I pray the Lord my soul to take. If I should die before I wake, I pray the Lord my soul to take. If I should die before I wake, I pray the Lord my soul to take. If I should die before I wake, I pray the Lord my soul to take. If I should—'

He woke up.

Joel sat up, gasping in air that felt as cool as ice water as it flooded his lungs. The dream refused to leave him, the boy's hushed voice still echoing in his ears. *If I should die before I wake, I pray the Lord my soul to take. If I should die before I wake—*

He told himself to stop it – he was awake already! But the thought seemed to have no power against the relentless chant. He had known that children's bedtime prayer for years, without really remembering where from. Only now, in the silence of the early morning and with the dream lingering on in the darkness, did the final words seem to take on new menace.

It was a protective chant, but he knew without questioning himself that it hadn't protected that little boy. He'd probably still been repeating it when the cupboard door had been suddenly flung open, and—

And . . . what? His mind provided no shape to the swell of terror that rose up to choke him, but that blankness was somehow worse than giving it a face.

He's coming after you, oh he's coming, and you can't run 'cos he'll catch up and you can't hide 'cos he'll find you and when he does he'll—

Joel threw himself out of bed and ran over to the light switch. He thumped it to flood the room with light, but that wouldn't quell the terror building in his chest. He kept telling himself there was no one there, but his own words made him feel no safer than the whispered prayer down in the dark.

If he had been just a few years younger, if he had been at home, he would have crawled in to see his mother and his sister and banished the nightmares with human warmth. But he wasn't a baby any more, and this wasn't their cramped little flat in the city, and it wasn't just him and Mum and Cassie any more.

So instead, he returned to his bed to grab a pillow, and hugged it to his chest as he sat with his back against the door, waiting for morning to come.

By the time Joel would normally be getting up, the unreasoning terror of the night had died down – but not totally. He still had a jittering, nervous feeling in his belly, the kind of anxiety he always got when he had to do something important in front of a crowd of people. The feeling that something bad was almost certain to happen, though he didn't know what or when.

Combined with the gritty eyes and dullness of not getting enough sleep, it made him oddly light-headed as he stumbled downstairs. Ignoring his sister, who was sitting on the back step eating an apple, he poured cereal into a bowl and slumped into the nearest chair.

'Earth to Joel,' said Cassie, when he didn't respond to her. 'Come in, Joel, what planet are you on?' Despite everything, she sounded considerably more cheerful than he did.

Joel groaned, defeated by the effort of raising a spoonful of cereal to his mouth. 'God, I'm knackered.'

'Didn't sleep?'

'Hardly at all.' It was on the tip of his tongue to tell her about the nightmares, but then he thought that she'd probably make a cheap joke about the Wilders. She seemed happier this morning, and now was not the time to burst that bubble. He blinked at her. 'You look cheerful. What is this, *Invasion of the Body Snatchers*?'

Cassie pulled a face at him. 'I've decided,' she announced, taking a bite out of her apple, 'to adopt a whole new attitude.'

'You're going to be nice to them?'

She just looked at him. 'Get real. No, I have decided . . . to pretend they don't exist.'

'Oh, that's mature,' he sniped. Lack of sleep and

the edgy feeling that something else might happen at any moment were making him grumpy.

'Works for me.' She shrugged, tossing the apple core into the bin. 'They are nothing, they are unimportant, they are . . . bugs to be squished under my shoe. No matter what they do, I will smile sweetly and completely ignore them.'

'You couldn't smile sweetly if you tried,' Joel pointed out.

'Then I'll have to go with evil smirks instead,' she said, demonstrating. Joel couldn't help grinning back. Life was so much easier when Cassie was in a good mood.

'Let's watch TV,' she decided. They only had a portable TV at the moment, a fuzzy little thing that didn't hold the picture very well – Gerald was going to have to go climbing on the roof to put up an aerial before they could get a proper set in there. It was currently standing on top of a box in what was going to be the front room, in amongst various dustsheets and abandoned tools.

Joel took his breakfast with him and they both lay sprawled out on their bellies, like they would have done back in the flat. Cassie punched buttons until she managed to find some film about a heroic dog, the only alternative to breakfast news and talk shows.

'Ten quid says he rescues somebody from an abandoned mineshaft before the end of the movie,' Cassie suggested.

'I say it'll be a burning building. And anyway, you haven't got ten quid.'

'Neither have you, so we're quits.' Frowning, she leaned forward and poked the portable aerial a few times. It didn't do much to improve the picture. 'Stupid useless TV. Trust Gerald.'

'Gerald who? I don't know any Gerald.' The lame joke still made Cassie smile, but at the same time it made Joel feel guilty. He thought the Wilders were OK. Why should he have to put them down to be with Cassie, or go against Cassie to hang out with Damon and Tim? It was a mess from all angles.

They lazed around in front of the TV, Joel glad to have it as a distraction, and Cassie probably just spacing out. Their mother came in to check on them a little while later. 'Joel. Cassie,' she said, doing that slightly brittle thing she did when she was fairly sure

Cassie was in an explosive mood. Joel winced in preparation, but his sister surprised him.

'Hi, Mum!' she said breezily. 'What are you doing today?' She sounded the way she always had when it had been just the three of them.

Their mother looked as if she didn't know whether to be pleased or suspicious. 'Morning, Cassie,' she said uncertainly. 'Why are you so cheerful all of a sudden?'

'I've decided to get a whole new attitude,' she said. Fortunately, she refrained from elaborating about the 'pretend they don't exist' part.

Their mother blinked a few times, but decided to let it ride. 'OK. Um, good. Gerald and I are going down to the shops this morning – do you two want to come?'

Joel looked to Cassie. Her face tightened for a moment, but she cleared it with an effort and said, 'No, that's OK, Mum. We'll stay here. We're watching a film.'

'Yeah, what she said,' Joel added.

'All right. If that's what you want.' Normally their mother would be pushing for them to come with her and make an effort, but today she probably thought

Cassie's good mood was more luck than she could ask for. 'We'll be going in a few minutes. The boys are upstairs; I think they're still in bed.'

'OK,' said Joel, wondering if Tim had also been woken in the middle of the night by threatening dreams.

A short while later their mother called out to them that she and Gerald were leaving. They both grunted in acknowledgement, and kept watching the stupid movie. Joel was too tired to try and think of something better to do with his time.

'Hey, Joel.' He looked up as Tim smiled at him tentatively from the door. The younger boy eyed Cassie warily, but she kept her gaze locked firmly on the television.

'Hey, Tim.' He hoped he wasn't about to get a load of grief from Cassie for not jumping on the 'pretend they don't exist' bandwagon. Even if he'd wanted to, he was too polite to do something like that. It was just his basic nature to get along with people.

'Hi.' Still keeping an eye on Cassie as if she was some kind of dangerous animal, Tim cautiously lowered himself down to sit by Joel. 'What're you watching?' he asked quietly.

'Dunno. Some animal movie. It's a bit rubbish.' He hadn't really been paying attention anyway; he kept zoning out, on the edge of falling asleep but not quite doing it.

'Can we watch the cartoons, then?' suggested Tim hopefully.

Joel glanced at his watch. 'Sure, yeah, I guess.' He looked over at his sister, who was completely ignoring the conversation. 'Cass, can we change the channel? The cartoons are on.'

'I'm watching this,' she said, not looking round at him.

'But it's rubbish,' he objected. If it had been his idea and not Tim's to change the channel, he knew she would have done it without even thinking. She didn't really care that much about watching the film, and she'd probably rather have the cartoons on anyway. It was all so stupid.

'I'm still watching it,' insisted Cassie sharply. Joel was ready to argue, but Tim stopped him.

'It's OK.' He shrugged.

'It's not.' They both looked up to see Damon in the doorway, scowling. 'You're only doing this 'cos he wants to watch something different,' he accused Cassie fiercely. 'You don't even want to watch the stupid movie! You're just doing it to spite us. That's the only reason you ever do anything, and I'm sick of it.'

Cassie ignored him too, but Damon wasn't as passive as his little brother. He strode across the room and poked her in the side with his foot. 'Hey! I'm talking to you.'

Cassie rolled over and sat up. 'Who invited you, moron?' She scowled.

'Moron? *I'm* not the one who's screwing up my own life to annoy other people.'

'*I'm* screwing up my life?' she demanded furiously. '*You're* the one screwing it up, idiot-boy. You and your dumb brother, *and* your dad.'

'Hey!' Damon gave her an angry shove. 'Why don't you leave my brother alone, psycho?'

'Hey yourself!' Never mind the fact that he was several centimetres taller and stronger, Cassie shoved him right back. 'Why don't you leave *me* alone, all of you? I never asked to come here!'

'Well, we never asked for you to come!' They were face to face now and yelling loudly.

'We were *fine* until you came along!' Cassie shouted. 'We never needed you, we never needed your brother, and we sure as hell don't need stupid *Gerald.*'

'Yeah? Well *I* don't need a little sister who gets some kind of kick out of messing everything up for the rest of us!'

Cassie blew her top. She thumped him in the chest with a fist and bellowed, 'Don't you *dare* say that! Don't you *dare* call me your sister, ever!'

'I wouldn't want you to be!'

'Yeah, well I'd rather *die!*'

As she stamped her foot in rage, it suddenly seemed to Joel that the entire room *exploded.*

All the doors and windows flew open as one, slamming into the walls with incredible force. The curtains were thrown up and the dustsheets billowed. The lights went off, and the picture on the TV fuzzed into a snowstorm of static.

In the sudden stillness there was no sound but their mingled breathing and the loud hum of the television.

Tim's eyes were wide with shock. 'What was that?' he asked uncertainly.

Damon, looking around the room warily, seemed no less nervous, but when he spoke his voice was as confident as ever. 'Wind,' he said quickly. 'It must have been a strong gust of wind.' He moved over to the windows to wrestle them closed again.

'Yeah, it was a mini hurricane,' retorted Cassie sarcastically. The room's double doors bounced uneasily in their frame, still settling back into place after being so violently thrown open. 'Zipped in here, through the doors and out the other side.

Yeah, that was really the wind, Damon.'

'Then what the hell else was it?' he demanded.

In the silence that followed Tim said very quietly, 'Ghosts.'

All was still as the whispered suggestion sank in, and then Damon straightened up and broke the moment. 'What's with all the crazy talk, kid?' he demanded, ruffling his brother's hair. 'It's nothing, Timmy – this house is in a state, and if the weather's been getting in, the whole place could be warped out of shape. You probably got like a – a funnel effect or something with the wind. It's not ghosts.'

Tim didn't look convinced, but he looked up at his brother and said, 'OK,' softly. As the two of them went out of the room together, Joel almost wished he had a big brother to reassure him like that.

Instead, he only had Cassie, and they'd always been too close in age to make much of the big-sister/little-brother thing. They looked at each other. Then Cassie snorted, 'Ghosts! Kid's a total basket case. Frightened of his own shadow.'

Joel shook his head. 'I'm not sure, Cassie.

Something . . . there's something not right here.' He gathered himself. 'Last night, I thought I saw—'

'Oh, relax.' His sister dismissed his concerns before he could even finish voicing them. 'The only horrible thing haunting this house is Damon Wilder.' She switched the TV off and on again, and the picture returned. 'Stupid aerial,' she grumbled.

She looked around to make sure Damon and Tim had gone, and grinned at Joel conspiratorially. 'Hey. *Now* we can watch the cartoons.'

Joel wasn't exactly happy about staying in that room, and yet at the same time he didn't think he'd feel safer anywhere else in the house. His bedroom back home in the flat had been a place of safety and sanctuary; his bedroom here was an echoing space full of nightmares. He wished his mother and Gerald were back.

When they ran out of cartoons, he went into Cassie's room and sat around doing nothing much while she read. She seemed quite pleased to have the company, although whether that was because she too felt nervous or because it was evidence he was on her side, Joel couldn't tell.

Finally, when half of the afternoon had rolled by and Mum and Gerald *still* hadn't returned, Joel was forced to leave the relative safety of Cassie's company and venture downstairs for food.

He found Damon in the kitchen, apparently having had the same idea. 'Hey, I'm making sandwiches. You want some?'

'Please,' he agreed gratefully. 'Where's Tim?' he asked as Damon tossed a few more slices of bread onto a plate.

'Upstairs. He didn't want to come down.' Damon jerked an eyebrow towards the room where they'd been watching TV, and Joel shivered uneasily.

'You think he's got a point?' he asked awkwardly.

'Ghosts?' To his surprise, now that he was no longer with his little brother Damon didn't seem so quick to be sceptical. 'I don't know, man. I didn't want to scare Tim, but hell . . . that was something.'

'It wasn't wind,' Joel agreed.

The older boy shook his head slowly. 'It couldn't have been. I don't see how it could.' He paused in spreading butter to frown pensively. 'And that thing with the cupboard last night. That was pretty nuts.'

'I've been seeing . . . weird things,' Joel confessed. 'Like, out of the corner of my eye, just for a moment. Things seem to move, or – or look different.'

Damon nodded slowly, then tossed the wrapped block of butter up in the air and caught it. 'I'm thinking it's got something to do with your sister,' he said unexpectedly.

'Cassie?' Joel frowned in confusion. 'What? It couldn't have been. She was in the room with us the whole time.'

'I know. I think it's her . . . but I don't think she knows she's doing it. Have you ever heard of a poltergeist?'

'Sure. Ghosts that throw things,' said Joel.

'Exactly. Well, I used to be into all that supernatural stuff, and I read a lot of books. D'you know what's usually present in houses where they have trouble with poltergeists? A teenage girl. Especially,' he said pointedly, 'an *over-emotional* teenage girl.'

'You think my sister's throwing stuff around with her mind?' Joel screwed his face up. 'OK, that's just crazy.'

Of course it was crazy. As he took his plate of

sandwiches back upstairs, he glanced at her lying slumped on her bed reading. His big sister, a centre of ghostly activity? As if. And anyway, whatever craziness was going on in this house, he was positive it had been there long before the six of them came marching in and tried to call this place a home.

Cassie looked up at him and saw the sandwiches. 'Oh my God, you learned how to make food!' she said, clutching at her heart as if the shock would kill her.

'Actually, Damon made them,' Joel admitted. He offered her the plate. 'You want one?' Cassie turned her nose up, so he took a bite out of one himself. 'Hey, Cass, they're not *poisoned*.'

She shrugged indifferently, but a few moments later her hand stole out to filch one off the plate.

'Oh, so it's a different story when you're hungry, is it?' he teased gently.

She shrugged at him. 'Damon doesn't exist. Therefore he couldn't have made sandwiches. Simple.'

'Oh, he existed quick enough when you were shouting at him this morning.'

'He started it!' she flared defensively.

'Somebody else ended it.' Joel remembered the shock of that sudden explosion of motion. He hesitated. 'Cass . . . do you really think there could be such a thing as ghosts?'

'Ghosts?' She put down her book and looked at him. 'Come on, Joel. How old are you? Seven?'

'No, but . . .' He shrugged uncomfortably. 'I don't know, it's just . . . This morning, and last night when we nearly got trapped in the loft, and the stuff getting thrown all over the garden and your room and – I don't like this house.' He looked around uneasily. 'I *really* don't like this house. I keep seeing and hearing stuff that's only half there.'

She frowned at him. 'You're creeping yourself out, J. It's just a house. You got trapped in the loft? So what if you did? There isn't a set of hinges in this house that doesn't need oiling. Gerald still hasn't finished unsticking the front door. And that's got to be used a hell of a lot more than the loft.'

Joel shook his head emphatically. 'No, you don't get it. It was *really* freaky, I'm telling you. Damon shut his brother in this cupboard up there, and it wouldn't open with all three of us trying – and then

I went in there, and the door just slammed by itself, and it was like this hand came out and—'

But Cassie had stopped listening the second he mentioned Damon's part in it all. 'Oh, well, there you go. Damon Wilder. He probably rigged the whole thing up with hidden wires and stuff.'

'I *really* don't think so, Cass. You weren't up there. You didn't feel what it was like.' He clenched his hands into frustrated fists. 'What if there *are* ghosts here, Cassie? Is that so totally impossible? What if there really are?'

Cassie shrugged and raised her eyebrows at him. 'If there are – well, hey, cool. A genuine chance to communicate with the dead – you don't think that would be awesome?'

He hoped his shudder of fear didn't show on the surface. 'Not really, no.'

'Oh, come on! If there were ghosts here and we figured out how to talk to them, it would be the coolest thing ever.'

'Cassie—' He was saved from trying to choke out just how bad an idea he thought that was by the sound of the door below. 'Hey, that's Mum.' He quickly scrambled downstairs to meet her – and escape the disturbing notion of trying to attract the attention of whatever it was that had invaded his dreams.

'Joel! Cassie.' Their mother smiled at them, loaded down with bags of paint and DIY supplies. 'You couldn't take one of these, could you?' They each grabbed one; unfortunately, that meant that when Gerald came in through the back door, Cassie was unable to beat a quick retreat.

'Hey there, Joel,' he smiled. 'Hiya, Cassie.'

'Hi, Gerald.'

'Yeah,' mumbled Cassie as coolly as she could get away with.

Refusing to be dismayed, Gerald smiled at her and moved towards the next room. 'Hey, I was hoping you'd come down. Listen, I've been going through that box of old papers I found down in the cellar – thought you two might want to take a look.'

'Oh, cool.' Joel tried to generate enthusiasm on his sister's part by sheer willpower, but it didn't work.

'No thanks,' she said curtly, and left as soon as she'd deposited the bag.

Gerald looked tired for a moment, then shrugged and gave Joel a wry grin. 'Well, at least she said thanks.'

'I'd like to look, though,' he said quickly and awkwardly. The bright smile of gratitude he got back made him feel better and worse at the same time. It was easy to really resent his sister at times.

He was glad that Gerald didn't linger while he was looking through the contents of the box; the ancient, damp-smelling papers had a certain curiosity value, but he knew he wouldn't get as much out of them as Cassie would. He was nervous about picking things up, let alone unfolding them, in case the old paper should crack or tear.

Most of it was only old receipts and invoices, anyway, the kind of dull business-like paperwork that got shoved in a file somewhere in case it needed to be consulted years down the line. It was all for building work in the early fifties: the original construction of the house, he guessed. Stuff that might be interesting to Gerald, or even to Cassie with her love of random little historical details like this, but not exactly a thrill a minute.

There were also a few old newspaper clippings, in even more fragile a state than the rest of the paperwork. Joel had hoped they would prove a bit more exciting, but found himself disappointed. They too mostly related to building of the house, which had apparently been quite a big deal in a village as small as this. The wealthy architect that Cassie had mentioned was named as a Mr Patrick Sanderson, but the newspapers seemed to have had little more to say about him, and most of the clippings just repeated the same information.

The last of the articles included, however, turned out to be about a wedding. Sanderson had married the widowed sister of one of the carpenters working on the house, a woman called Victoria Hawkins. Joel had got the impression from Cassie and the lack of detail in the news that he must have been a bit of an eccentric recluse, but perhaps the fact that he was rich had outweighed that in the widow's eyes.

Joel was vaguely curious to know how long the Sandersons had lived in the house, but the box's contents only seemed to go up to the completion of the building work. The only other thing of interest was some black and white photographs, most of them shots of the building work that didn't include any people. There was one that might have been Sanderson, a man sitting at a desk with his head at the wrong angle for the photo to clearly show his face. Another one showed a pretty woman sitting smiling in the garden. Victoria Hawkins?

He thought perhaps he'd emptied the box now, but tilted it up to find one last picture face down at the bottom. Joel prised it out and turned it over – and stopped breathing.

The face that stared up from the long-ago photograph was instantly familiar.

The photograph showed two skinny, dark-haired boys standing rather awkwardly in the garden: one about eleven or twelve years old, the other considerably younger. They were both squinting against the sun, and the picture quality wasn't really very good. It was clear enough, however, for Joel to be absolutely positive that he'd seen the older boy before.

Which was nonsense, of course, because this black and white photo was decades old, and both boys would be old men if he saw them today. And yet . . .

He *had* seen that face, and seen it more than once.

On a terrified boy literally running for his life out in the garden . . . and reflected in a mirror that no one was looking into but himself.

Joel forced himself to breathe out. No. This was nonsense. His fevered imagination was drawing things together that didn't really match. The face of the boy in the picture was rendered indistinct thanks to the sun, so naturally Joel had mentally associated him with a boy whose features he'd barely been able to see thanks to the rain and lightning. That didn't mean they were actually the same − or that something he thought he'd seen in a mirror when half frightened out of his wits had any connection to either of them.

There. That was a good, strong, logical explanation.

So why didn't he believe a word of it?

There was nothing on the photograph that would give identifying information, and no clue in the paperwork about any connection the boys might have with the house. He remembered Cassie had seemed to know something about the history of the house when they'd spoken the night before. He took the photograph upstairs with him, and knocked gently on the doorframe.

'Hey, Cass. You know that rich weirdo who built this place? Patrick Sanderson, right?'

She frowned. 'Yeah, sounds right. Why?'

'I was just wondering . . . do you know if he had kids?'

His sister shrugged theatrically. 'I have absolutely *no* idea.' She eyed him curiously. 'Weird question, J. What's up?'

'Oh, I – I just found this photo in that box of stuff Gerald brought up from the cellar. It's all from back when the house was first built, so I just wondered if they were his sons or something.'

Tim came up behind him in the hallway, looking curious. 'Who might be whose sons?'

'This picture I found. I'm trying to find out who these two boys are – I thought they might be related to the guy who built the place or something.'

Joel flashed the picture at him, and Tim gasped in shock.

'What?' Cassie demanded.

Tim gripped Joel's arm rather tightly. 'I've seen that boy before,' he said slowly.

Joel stared at him. 'You too?'

'Him too what?' Cassie was plainly lost.

Joel took a deep breath. 'Cassie . . . I think this boy might be the ghost that we've been seeing.'

She made a disparaging noise. 'Oh, Lord, you're not still going on about the ghost thing?'

'Cass, I'm serious! I really have – I've been seeing some weird stuff, OK? Blood on the floor, strange reflections . . . I've been having all these really vivid nightmares—'

It was Tim's turn to look at him in surprise. 'You've been having them too? The – the trying to run away – up there in that cupboard, the *chanting*—'

'Yes!' Joel didn't know whether to be triumphant or horrified. If Tim was having the same dreams, that meant he *wasn't* going crazy, and that meant—

He turned to his sister. 'Cassie, you've got to believe us. This house is haunted. There's something going on here.'

She shook her head at the pair of them. 'You know what? Fine. You guys really think there's a ghost here? Then let's prove it. If this kid's spirit is trying to talk to us, we should talk back. Let's do a séance.'

Joel gulped. 'Cassie—'

'Unless you're *scared*,' she said pointedly.

'I'm scared,' admitted Tim frankly. Joel wondered if that didn't, in a twisted way, make Tim actually braver than he was. Joel was pretty scared too, but he would rather die than tell Cassie that.

'Oh, you're such a *wuss*,' said Cassie scathingly. 'You won't do it then? Why don't you just go running back to Daddy – ask him to—'

'Oh, we'll do it.' Damon gave her a smug smile from the doorway. 'We can take on your stupid séance *any* day.'

Joel wondered when this had become the house gathering point. Damon must have wandered over to see where his little brother had got to – at just the wrong time.

Now it was Tim's turn to make a dismayed face and try to interrupt. 'Damon—'

'You think you're so hard,' Damon said to Cassie, ignoring his brother. 'I guarantee you'll be running off screaming before either of us will.' Joel doubted that. Cassie could be brash, rude and stubborn, but she was every bit as tough as she acted. 'Name the time and place, sis, we'll be there.'

'Call me that again, and there'll be *two* ghosts haunting this place,' she warned him. She gave her best evil smile and spoke lightly. 'OK, then. Up in the loft; midnight.'

'Midnight?' Joel didn't like the sound of that at all. This house creeped him out enough during the day, let alone at night when his nightmares ran wild.

'Shut up, Joel.' Cassie's attention was focused solely on Damon.

His arrogant smirk, the match of hers, didn't falter. 'Oh, we'll show up. If *you* do.'

She got right in his face. 'Wouldn't miss it for the world,' she said sweetly.

'See you there, then.' He shrugged, and stepped back from her. 'Come on, Tim,' he called. His little brother scrambled to join him, shooting Joel one last glance of sympathetic anxiety.

Then Joel was left alone with Cassie. He pulled a dismayed face as she sat down beside him. 'Cassie, I really don't think we should do this . . .'

'Oh, come on,' she punched him on the shoulder. 'It's not *real*. It's just a game, like that party thing where you blindfold people and make them touch stuff that feels really icky. I'm just trying to freak them out.' She grinned brightly at him. 'Actually, I don't even know *how* to do a proper séance or anything,' she confessed.

He frowned. 'But you said—'

'Oh, I can fake it. You get some letters, you get a glass and move it around – easy. It's not the same as using a proper Ouija board or anything. So even if there *are* ghosts, it wouldn't actually work.'

'You think?' he said hopefully.

'I'm sure. Who am I, Gypsy Rose? I can't contact the dead!'

'So it's all just a big practical joke then?'

'Yeah. We can make it really creepy and stuff, and totally freak them out, and then I'll sneak up behind Damon and grab him in the dark or something.' She grinned at the thought. 'I'm going to make him cry like a little girl.'

'Some little girl other than you, this would be?' he wondered.

'Girl? Me?' Cassie flexed her muscles in a body-builder pose. 'I am woman! Hear me roar!' Joel laughed.

The amusement didn't last long, however. Once he was back in his own room without company to distract him, a thought that had been nagging at the back of his mind insisted on resurfacing.

Cassie said it was all a fake, and it wouldn't work because she didn't know how to do it properly. They couldn't contact the dead because she didn't know how to reach them. But what if the ghosts on the other side were trying just as hard to reach *back* . . . ?

Joel wasn't looking forward to the midnight hour *at all*.

XII

Joel went to bed that evening with a horrible tight feeling in his stomach. He was nearly certain – indeed he almost prayed – that he wouldn't fall asleep before midnight. But somehow he still did.

He was running again, running through the garden. Except that it wasn't overgrown like it was now; everything was neatly planted and cut back like in the old photographs, and there was nowhere to *hide* . . .

He raced through the garden and vaulted a row of plants in pots, kicking one over in a spray of earth.

He stumbled and fell flat on his face, but pushed himself straight back up again, knowing there was no time to risk delaying. No time, because *it* was gaining on him.

It? He? She? Someone . . . Someone he knew – he was sure it was someone he knew, but with murderous intent and the heavy, ragged breathing of an enraged animal. *Please, just let me get away. Please, just let me get away* . . .

The rear fence loomed like a safe haven. *If only I can get out – out into the village, somebody can save me* . . . He threw himself at the fence, but it was slippery, his hands wouldn't grip it, and suddenly he was being seized by the ankle and pulled backwards—

'Joel!'

He was jerked out of the nightmare and into a sitting position in one sharp motion. There was a dark shape in his room, hanging over him, and he was opening his mouth to scream or maybe just gasp desperately, when an urgent hand suddenly covered it.

'Joel, you idiot. It's me.'

Joel's brain took a break from pumping out

terror-signals to translate the silhouette and the hissed voice into his sister Cassie. She let him go and he breathed in and out raggedly, trying to slow his heart. What would have happened, what awful thing might he have seen, if she hadn't pulled him out of the dream right at that very moment?

If you die in your dreams, you don't wake up. He remembered being told that once, and thinking it was stupid because no one could possibly know. But that kind of thinking was for daylight. Right now, all he knew was that it was dark and his heart was beating so fast it hurt.

The whites of Cassie's eyes flashed in the darkness. 'Come on, Joel, get up. It's nearly midnight!' she said, shaking him.

'*Come on!*' She shook him again when he didn't respond. He was gripping his bedcovers in rigid hands, and he couldn't seem to make his muscles untighten. Was this what people meant when they said 'frozen with terror'? The sweat on his back certainly felt like ice.

Losing patience, Cassie simply tugged the covers off him. 'Joel, I'm not letting you chicken out of this.

We are *not* letting Damon Wilder get the better of us.'

As what little security the bedcovers provided was yanked away from him, Joel could suddenly move again. He rolled unwillingly out of bed, not wanting to do this, but not keen to be left alone to go back to his dreams either. He grabbed a pair of socks to put on as a delaying tactic, hoping that feeling less undressed would make him a bit less unsettled. It didn't really help.

It felt strange to be out of his bed at night, let alone to be on his way to a midnight séance. Cassie was the trouble-maker; Joel was the kind of boy who always followed the rules, even silly little ones like making sure you walked on the left in the corridors in school. It was just his nature.

There'd be hell to pay if their mother caught them sneaking about this late, but that was the least of Joel's worries. Being yanked out of the middle of his nightmare like that had got him even more on edge, and this time there wasn't the reassurance of morning sunlight to turn to. The upstairs of the house was as dark as if he'd gone blind.

Even as he followed Cassie, he was trying to send

psychic messages to the Wilder boys: *Chicken out – oversleep – trip over and wake everybody up* . . . Unlike Cassie, he had no interest in seeing them put down or humiliated – he just did *not* want to have to do this.

He didn't think Damon or Cassie understood. Tim did, but Tim could no more control his big brother than Joel could order Cassie around. The two of them were determined to go ahead with this, because they thought it was a game – just playing at dares. Even if they could feel some lesser shadow of the atmosphere that the younger boys sensed in the house, they didn't take it seriously enough, didn't understand how dangerous it could get. During the day Joel might have his doubts, but now, at midnight, he was certain: there was something very, very wrong about this house.

However, his mental messages to the Wilder brothers didn't get through. A gleam of yellow light under the bedroom door betrayed their presence. Beside him in the dark, Cassie shook her head. 'Amateurs,' she whispered to Joel. 'If *I'd* been up first, I'd've kept the lights off and then jumped out on them when they came in.'

'That's because you're evil,' Joel whispered back, and decided he was glad the Wilders hadn't been the ones to come and get them. Giving poor Tim a heart attack wouldn't exactly be his idea of fun.

As Cassie pushed the door open, his eyes were flooded with light, and he had to blink furiously until he could see. He had thought that it would be reassuring, but instead he just felt dread well up somewhere deep in his belly. This was it. They were here, and Cassie was really going to do this.

'You came,' said Damon, at normal volume, raising his eyebrows.

'Jeez, wake the whole house, why don't you?' said Cassie, quickly pulling the door to behind them. 'Or was that the plan? Switch on all the lights, make some noise and hope Daddy comes along to rescue you?'

Damon shrugged. 'We're not scared.' Joel thought he was speaking for himself there; he exchanged a sympathetic glance with Tim, who looked as sick as he felt inside.

The older boy led the way out onto the landing, easing down the ladder carefully to minimize the noise. 'Ladies first,' he said with an elaborate bow and a mocking smile. Cassie sneered right back, and swung herself up without hesitation.

Joel and Tim followed, and they both flinched as the faint light from the bedroom below was suddenly cut off. Damon came up after them, moving a little clumsily in the dark. He set something on the floor beside the hatch, and when it clicked and light blazed into life, Joel realized it was a table lamp. 'Extension flex,' Damon said smugly, and slid the hatch almost closed.

It was very cramped in there with the four of them. In the lamplight Joel could see that the ceiling was slanted, following the shape of the roof, he guessed: high towards the wall with the cupboard and getting progressively lower. Where he was sitting, he would have got a nasty crack if he'd straightened up too fast.

Damon looked across at Cassie. 'You bring the stuff?'

'Sure.' Joel could now see that she had her school bag in her hand. She pulled out a bunch of ragged paper squares held together with an elastic band.

'What's that?' frowned Tim.

'Letters, you idiot.' Cassie quickly whipped off the

band and dealt the felt-penned letters of the alphabet out in a wide circle. Then she produced a glass – one of the clear tumblers from the kitchen – and put it upside-down in the centre of the circle.

Damon rolled his eyes. 'Oh, this is so lame.'

'Scared?' accused Cassie immediately. He sneered at her mockingly. 'Then let's do this.' They all scrambled over to sit around the circle.

'W-what do we do?' asked Tim in a low voice.

'Reach out and put your hand on the glass,' Cassie directed. 'Lightly; just your fingertips.' They all leaned forward to do as she directed. The smooth glass felt as cold as ice beneath Joel's fingers, and despite the bright, warm lamp not far from his elbow, he suddenly felt as if he was surrounded by shadows. He wanted to call the whole thing off, but it felt too late, as if to call an end to it now would be worse than carrying on.

They'd made a magic circle. Every horror or fantasy story he'd ever read had the same thing to say about magic circles: you weren't supposed to break them. It would all go disastrously wrong if you broke them.

128

So he said nothing, and they all stayed still for a moment. Finally, Damon let out a quiet snort of amusement.

'Shut up.' Cassie looked up at the ceiling, though there was nothing up there but cobwebs and damp stains. 'Is there anybody there?' she asked firmly. Damon snorted again. 'Shut *up*.' The brief pause that followed was painfully oppressive.

'Is there anybody there? Can you hear us?' Cassie asked again. Her voice had taken on a deeper tone, the one she had used when she was on stage in a school play years ago, doing the narration. Then it had been almost comical; now it was creepy.

After a moment there was a soft, very soft scrape of glass on wood. They all looked down, and Tim let out a tiny little gasp. The tumbler had started to move.

XIII

Joel's breath caught in his throat as the glass under his fingertips began to scrape along the wooden boards. It slid across the circle, their hands following it, and came to rest by the scrawled letter C.

'C,' said Cassie aloud, eyes suddenly wide. The glass returned to the centre of the circle, then moved over to the letter D.

'C, D.' For a second Joel was confused; what did CDs have to do with anything? And then it hit him. 'Cassie Demetrius!' Beside him, his sister's shoulders suddenly tightened. She wasn't quite so sceptical now.

Cassie softly sounded out the letters as the moving glass picked them out, one by one. 'S . . . T . . . I . . . N . . . K— *Damon!*'

The older boy exploded into a guffaw as a furious Cassie launched herself across the circle to attack him. Damon scrambled to his feet and danced backwards towards the corner, fending her off with his hands. 'I had you!' he crowed. 'I *so* had you!'

'Damon!' Even Tim sounded furious. 'Don't be such a *jerk.*'

Joel didn't speak, still catching his breath shakily. Stupid, stupid, stupid, how could they ever have fallen for a dumb trick like that—?

There was a sudden scratching sound. His heart stopped, and his eyes flickered to the glass, abandoned in the centre of the circle. They'd all let go when Cassie launched herself at Damon. Had it . . . ? No, of course it hadn't, he was freaking out, and it was all Damon's fault—

It *moved.* As Joel stared at it, the glass jerked a tiny fraction of an inch. Then another. Joel looked up, across the circle, and met Tim's eyes. They stared at each other, then back down at the glass.

'Cassie.' His voice was barely more than a whisper, nowhere near loud enough to be heard above Damon's muffled laughter and Cassie's indignant squawking. He licked his lips and tried again. '*Cassie!*'

'Damon!' said Tim at the same time.

'What?' Damon, still laughing, grabbed Cassie's wrists to keep her from hitting him, and turned back to the two of them. Then he froze. The glass was moving again.

Cassie followed his gaze and let out a sudden gasp. Fight forgotten, she stood still, not even remembering to wrench herself free of his grip.

They all watched as the glass tumbler crawled at a snail's pace to the edge of the circle. E. Nobody was playing tricks on them now. Nobody was touching it at all.

The glass very gradually came to a halt; then, just as gradually, began moving in the opposite direction. Joel watched as it slid across the circle. 's,' they all said at the same time, as if the others somehow might not have noticed where it landed.

Was it his imagination, or did the glass move a little faster as it slid back across the floorboards? 'C.'

This time the glass simply slid sideways a little. 'A.' It was definitely getting faster. 'P.'

'*Escape*,' said Damon grimly, even as it made for the letter E. He was still gripping Cassie by the forearms, quite tightly now, but she didn't seem to object – or even notice.

By this point the upturned tumbler was moving rapidly, whipping across the rough boards like one of those movies where they slide drinks across the top of the bar. 'N. O.' Joel frowned. 'No? Was that wrong—?' He stopped abruptly as it continued to reel off letters. E – S – C – A – P – E. Then it came to a stop.

Escape. No escape.

Joel looked across the circle at Tim, who had an expression like a rabbit caught in car headlights. Suddenly he didn't want to be up in this loft any more.

Maybe thinking the same thing, Damon started to move out of the corner, tugging Cassie with him towards the ladder. 'Come on. We should—' He was abruptly interrupted by the zip of the glass moving across the boards at high speed. The scraps of paper actually fluttered with the wind of its passage.

The letters started coming, almost too fast to call

out, but not too fast for Joel to follow with his eyes:
I – F – I – S – H – O – U – L – D—

If I should die before I wake, I pray the Lord my soul to take. If I should die—

'– before I wake, I pray the Lord my soul to take. If I should die before I wake—' It took a moment to realize that the voice chanting the words aloud in a breathy whisper was his own; his own, and the echo just a fraction behind it was Tim's. He met the other boy's eyes, suddenly knowing that at some point in his own dark nightmares, Tim had been crushed down on his knees in that same closet, listening to that unceasing chant.

Joel didn't know what broke his paralysis. Maybe it was simply the rising sound of glass on wood as the tumbler moved faster and faster; maybe it was some feeling growing in the atmosphere . . . suddenly he was on his feet. 'Tim! Get back!'

The younger boy was scrambling up, and Damon grabbed his brother and literally pulled him away. The two of them and Cassie pressed back into the far corner as Joel threw himself backwards away from the circle . . .

The glass exploded into shards and they all cried out at once. In the same moment the lamp went out and Joel couldn't tell if the spray of glass fragments that struck his upraised arm came from the tumbler or the bulb.

'Damon!' Tim shrieked, but Joel couldn't figure out where his voice came from. He staggered backwards and thumped his head far too hard against the slope of the ceiling.

'Joel! Open the hatch!' Damon commanded, sounding tense but not as out-and-out panicked as his younger brother. Joel fumbled along the floor for the sliding handle, knowing it was right beside him but unable to find it.

Suddenly there was a click and a small circle of light blossomed to life. He glimpsed Damon across the room, holding up the torch. Looking back at the floor, he suddenly saw that his scrabbling fingers had been only a centimetre away from the handle they were seeking. He grabbed hold of it, and wrenched the hatch open.

Abruptly, as if the room had been full of water and he had pulled the plug, the oppressive atmosphere poured away. He didn't think there had been any noise beyond that initial explosion of glass, and yet his ears were ringing as if something incredibly loud had suddenly ceased. Whatever had been in the room with them, it was gone now.

That didn't stop him from throwing himself down the ladder as if he was on fire, or the others from barrelling after him.

The four of them halted at the end of the landing, all breathing heavily. Damon had one arm slung around his little brother's waist as if ready to lift him off the ground and carry him if he had to. His other hand was still on the small of Cassie's back, where he'd been pushing her along.

'You OK?' he asked her in a low voice.

Cassie somehow mustered enough presence of mind to scowl at him, though she didn't shake him off. 'Better than you,' she accused.

Damon just laughed, albeit shakily. 'You're probably right,' he agreed mildly. He tugged his brother closer and looked down at him. 'Tim?'

'I think I'm still alive,' said Tim, very wide-eyed. 'Joel?'

Although he might have expected to be spoken to, it took Joel a moment to collect his thoughts enough to answer. 'I, er . . . I guess I'm OK.'

'Yeah.' Damon let out a wobbly breath. 'Guess we . . . guess we were kind of wrong about the ghosts, huh?'

'You were wrong,' said Tim quietly. '*We* were right.'

Damon was opening his mouth to answer when they all jumped at the sound of thundering footsteps coming up the stairs. For a second Joel's heart caught in his chest, and then he recognized the tread.

'What in *God's name*—? Joel? Cassie?' Their mother came to an abrupt halt as she saw that they were all there. 'All of you? What on *earth* is going on up here?'

XIV

Their mother gave the four of them her angrily expectant look, the one with the arched eyebrows that you didn't dare disobey. Joel's tongue suddenly felt swollen and useless in his mouth as his instincts to confess all warred with a complete inability to think what to say.

Damon leaped into the gaping silence. 'Sorry, Amanda. It was a dare.'

'A dare,' said Joel's mother shortly, loading those two simple words with a world of disbelief and resigned disgust. She turned to her own two children. 'Cassie?'

Joel half expected her to quickly blame it on Damon and Tim, but she didn't. 'It was a dare, Mum,' she said quietly. Their mother regarded her for a long moment, then looked across to Joel. He could only shrug nervously, still tongue-tied.

She sighed heavily, and rubbed her eyes. 'All of you, back to bed, OK?' she said wearily. 'Now. Just – just go back to bed. That's all.' She turned round and stomped back down the stairs.

Joel pulled his pyjama shirt closer about himself, feeling bad for making his mother's life so difficult – and feeling really strange about thinking that was important at a time like this. Ghosts, he reminded himself: real ghosts, breaking things, sending messages, throwing things around! But it all seemed somehow muted by the intrusion of everyday life.

Damon must have been on the same wavelength, because he said, almost apologetically, 'We should go back to bed.'

'Go, then,' said Cassie pointedly. But she was only abrupt, not angry.

Damon nodded, looked about ready to say something, and then changed his mind. 'Come on, Tim.'

He chuckled slightly nervously and glanced towards the ceiling. 'Think I might just be grabbing the duvet and moving in up your end of the room tonight, if you don't mind.'

From the fervent way Tim nodded, Joel suspected he'd have forcibly dragged his brother over to join him if he'd tried to do anything else. He wasn't exactly looking forward to going back to his own echoing bedroom himself.

Cassie looked across at him. 'You going back to bed?'

He shrugged awkwardly. 'I guess.' What were they supposed to do? They were kids. They couldn't call out the ghost investigators or spend the night in a hotel or decide they would stay up all night. They just had to put up with it. They didn't have a choice.

For a moment he seriously wanted to run after his mother and tell her what had just happened. But how could he? What words could he possibly use to convince her of something he found so unbelievable himself?

Joel went back into his bedroom. He shut the door, hearing the echoing click as Cassie did the same to hers, and then he was once again alone.

As he stood there in the dark, the hairs on the back of his neck all bristled. An icy breeze stirred the curtains, and he couldn't tell if it was just from the window or something else.

'Who are you?' he asked, barely louder than a whisper. 'What do you want?'

There was no response, and somehow that was even worse than getting one. Joel tugged his quilt and pillows from the bed, and prepared for another sleepless night with his back pressed up against the door.

He must have dozed, or at least closed his eyes long enough to lose track of time, for when he opened them again it was daylight. His bedcovers were messily piled about him, and when he stood up he realized that he'd never got round to taking his socks off. As he dressed himself now, a number of tiny glass shards fell to the floor.

He went and knocked softly on his sister's door; she opened it immediately, fully dressed despite the early hour. He was willing to bet she hadn't slept so well either.

'Hey, Cass,' he said, leaning his head against the doorframe. She smiled weakly at him. 'Rough night?'

'Oh yeah,' she agreed, flicking her eyebrows up for emphasis.

'Did you dream?'

'Oh, that would involve having actually *gone to sleep*,' she pointed out.

'Yeah.' He hesitated. 'What do we do now?' It was a genuine question. Yesterday he had half believed that there were ghosts in this house – now all four of them were sure of it. But . . . what did they do now?

Cassie chewed her lower lip thoughtfully. 'We have to go back up there,' she said.

'Cass—'

She raised a hand to cut him off. 'Not to— Just to clean up. We have to get up there and clear up the glass and everything before Mum or Gerald sees it.' For once she was too preoccupied to make his name sound like another word for 'scum'. 'God knows what they're going to think we were up to if they see all that junk.'

'That doesn't seem right,' he said. Scurrying to clear up after themselves as if they'd done something wrong. 'Couldn't we—?'

143

'Do what?' she interrupted him. 'Tell Mum, "It wasn't us, the ghosts did it"? That ought to go down even better than "It wasn't me, it was the Wilders."' A trace of her previous bitterness crept back in.

'Yeah, and maybe the ghosts *did* do it. No, no, not last night.' He waved her down hurriedly. 'I mean your room, the wallpaper – could that all have been the same as what happened in there?' Which meant, he didn't add, that none of it had been Tim and Damon, and she'd been blaming them for something they hadn't even done. Just like she'd claimed their mother was doing to her.

For a moment Cassie looked troubled, and he knew the same thoughts must be passing through her head. Then she shrugged and frowned. 'Ah, hell, I don't know. Maybe it was. But it could just as easily have been Damon. He's a total jerk. I mean, look what he was doing with the glass last night.'

'He didn't think it was real,' Joel pointed out. 'Neither did you! We could've all been *killed* in there 'cos you two were playing about!'

Cassie gave him a sceptical look. 'Oh, J, you watch too many horror films. Ghosts don't kill people. You saw what was going on with the letters: it was trying to tell us something. We just have to find a way to figure out what.'

Joel raised his eyebrows disbelievingly. 'Yeah? I thought "No escape" was pretty self-explanatory, really.'

To that, Cassie had no reply.

The loft was less threatening with daylight spilling in from down below – but not completely so. Joel half fancied he felt a crackle like static across his skin as he and Cassie crawled around trying to collect up the shards of glass and paper. Whatever roamed the inside of this house, it was stronger here.

He couldn't get the muttered words of the boy's desperate prayer out of his head. Cassie said ghosts didn't kill people, but what did she know? She hadn't even believed in them yesterday.

'Hey.' Damon appeared at the top of the ladder a few moments later, and came along to help. Tim followed him up and joined the clean-up efforts without complaint, though he flinched nervously at every loud noise.

They worked mostly without speaking; finally the

room seemed to be clear, and Damon wadded up the bag of paper and glass fragments to stuff into his pocket.

'I'll just shove this in the skip with the rest,' he said. 'No one'll notice. Can somebody bring that lamp down?'

He went downstairs to the kitchen, and the younger three followed, unwilling to stay up there a moment longer than they had to. Cassie didn't even raise the slightest objection to tagging along with the Wilders. Fortunately, their mother and Gerald weren't up yet to remark on the weirdness of it.

The new, tentative truce lasted just about as long as it took them to cluster around the breakfast table.

'We need to find a way to talk to the ghost,' Cassie announced, tossing her apple up in the air and catching it before she took a bite.

Damon looked at her as if she was completely crazy. 'You what? Er, hello, were you *here* last night?'

'I don't want to do that again,' announced Tim, with feeling.

'I hear you.' Joel nodded.

Cassie shrugged. 'OK, so the séance wasn't such

146

a hot idea. How was I supposed to know it was going to be that powerful? But the ghost was trying to tell us something. Everyone knows spirits stick around because they have unfinished business. We have to help it.'

'Help it? What is this, an episode of *Scooby Doo*? That thing's dangerous! The way it was throwing stuff around, somebody could get seriously hurt!'

'Jeez, how old are you, sixty?' Cassie mocked. 'You sound like a little old lady. "Don't do that, dear, you might scrape your little knees." You boys are such cowards.'

'No, we're just not stupid,' retorted Damon defensively. 'You don't mess around with this stuff, Cassie – we're in way over our heads.'

Cassie could only shake her head in disgust. 'This is unbelievable. Listen to yourself! It's a *ghost*. A real, genuine, *actual* ghost, and you want to run away from it because it's a little bit scary?'

'It's a *lot* scary,' Tim said pointedly. 'You don't understand. You haven't been having the nightmares. There's something *wrong* here, something really really bad—'

'Ghosts are shadows,' said Cassie firmly. 'That's all they are, OK? And nightmares are even less than that. It's all in your head.'

'Last night wasn't in our heads!' objected Damon.

'For God's sake!' Cassie thumped the table in frustration. 'It was *trying to tell us something* – can't you idiots see that? It probably doesn't even know its own strength. Joel, tell them,' she commanded.

Joel wasn't sure *what* he was supposed to tell them, and he didn't have much of an appetite for his breakfast any more, either. 'I don't know,' he said. 'I don't – I just – I don't want to talk about this any more. Leave me alone.' He got up and stomped into the next room, sitting down with his back against the wall and closing his eyes. His head was swimming with confusion and nightmares and lack of sleep, and he didn't want to have to think about ghosts any more.

For a moment, at least, Cassie and Damon fell blessedly silent. Maybe it was the shock of hearing him actually speak up for himself. Hell, even Tim was sticking up for himself more than *he* was. Why did he always have to be the good one, the polite one? The one who always went along with what other people wanted?

When had that happened, exactly? Had it always been that way, or had he woken up one morning and suddenly decided that it was his job to be the peacemaker? It wasn't as if he could even blame it on some kind of genetic thing – not with a sister like Cassie. *She* never had any trouble saying what was on her mind.

Joel heard footsteps coming towards him across the hardwood floor: Cassie? Coming to apologize, or more likely to just try and badger him into agreeing with her side of things. 'I *said*, leave me alone.' He grimaced.

He opened his eyes . . . and saw that Cassie and the others were still in the other room. Slowly, very slowly, his eyes were drawn to the left.

There was a dark shadow on the wall beside him – a shadow with nothing to cast it. The slim silhouette of a boy, far clearer and more sharply defined than his own blurred outline. As if there was a boy he couldn't see, standing directly in front of him . . .

Joel screamed.

The shadow puffed out of existence as if it had never been, and the other three came scrambling towards him. 'J! What's wrong?' 'Joel! You OK? What happened?'

Joel slowly pushed himself up into a crouch, heart pounding in his chest. He scrambled for words, but for a moment could only gasp, sucking in breaths that chilled his lungs.

They all jumped as the door swung open behind them. It was Joel and Cassie's mother.

'Joel?' she asked worriedly. Her hair was untidy and her dressing gown only slung loosely round her,

151

as if she'd literally jumped right out of bed and come running. She took in the three of them standing over him. 'What's going on in here? Is everyone all right?'

Joel wasn't sure whether it was some childish feeling of security now that his mother in the room or just the urgent need to find a cover story that helped him regain a little of his composure. 'Yeah, I, um, I—' He swallowed. 'I just . . . there was a spider. Biggest spider you ever saw.' The shaky laugh that came out of his mouth was more to do with the fear still surging through his veins than any pretence at embarrassment. 'It ran right over my hand.'

Perhaps unsure whether this was a cover or the truth, Tim took the safer route and edged backwards. Cassie made a show of lifting things up and looking around. 'I wanna see it.'

Their mother heaved a weighty sigh, some of the annoyance of the previous night returning after it had been proved to be nothing serious. 'Well, fine, but can you try not to sound like you're being murdered next time? Honestly, I don't know what's got into you all. Charging around the house at all hours – I know you must all be feeling rather cooped up, but let's try to keep the hyperactivity down a bit, OK?'

Damon shot Joel a curious glance before straightening up and smiling apologetically. 'Sorry, Amanda. We really didn't mean to wake you.'

She gave him a grateful smile. 'No, Damon, that's quite all right. I was just getting up anyway; your father's starting on the cellar this morning.'

'Is he still thinking about enlarging it?'

'Well, I don't know. He seems to think it's rather small for a place this size, but if it was built that way originally . . .' Damon nodded. 'Anyway, he's going to take a look at the pipes first, and probably rebuild part of the doorframe. It's completely rotted out where the damp's been getting in there. I'm surprised the whole kitchen didn't collapse around his ears when he opened it up.'

'Great,' Cassie groaned. 'We're supposed to sit around and listen to him crashing around down there all day?'

Her mother shot her a look. 'Actually, Cassie, I was going to suggest that the four of you come into town with me and we all go and see a film.' Her tone of voice made it clear she was expecting her daughter, and possibly Damon as well, to be difficult as ever.

She was probably taken aback, then, by the immediate chorus of eager replies.

'Sure!'

'Can we?'

'Oh, cool—'

'OK.' Clearly, even Cassie was a lot more eager to get away from the atmosphere of this house than she was pretending.

Their mother eyed them all suspiciously, and then threw up her hands as if giving up on figuring them out. 'Well . . . OK then! You kids get your shoes on and I'll just go and get dressed.'

Joel didn't get a chance to speak to the others while she was hovering around, but he went into Cassie's room and sat on the edge of her bed while he laced his trainers.

'What did you see, J?' she asked him. 'I *know* you're not scared of spiders.'

'It was . . .' He let out something like a sigh, trying to ease the grip of tension on his chest. It didn't work.

'There was this boy. Standing right in front of me. Right there in the room with me.'

Cassie stopped messing with her hair and stared at him. 'You saw a ghost?'

He shifted uncomfortably. 'Not exactly, I – I had my eyes closed for a moment, and there were these footsteps, and I thought it was one of you – but then I looked round, and there was this . . . shadow. On the wall next to me, like he was standing right in front of me but I couldn't see him. And then it disappeared when I . . . er, yelled.' Screamed his head off, more like.

She sat down beside him, frowning thoughtfully. 'And you still think it's one of those boys from that picture?'

'Yeah.' He hadn't seen even an indistinct face this time, but he was still sure.

'Well, I guess it gives us somewhere to start. I wonder who they are?'

'I don't know.' Not strictly true. He was absolutely sure, whoever else they might be, that in his nightmares he'd been one of them as they hid together in that cupboard.

Cassie stood up and straightened out her collar. She pulled an exaggeratedly thoughtful face. 'Well, Watson, this case is getting more and more interesting.'

He finished with his laces. 'I think you mean "freaky",' he informed her wryly.

'Well, you say "potato"—'

'And so does everybody else I've ever met,' he pointed out. Cassie rolled her eyes.

Damon appeared in the doorway, his brother following behind. 'What's this?' he wondered.

'Joel saw a ghost,' Cassie supplied.

'The shadow of one,' he corrected. 'It was a kid about Tim's age. I didn't see his face, but I'm sure it's the boy from the photograph.'

'What photograph?' Damon looked puzzled, and Joel remembered he'd walked in on their discussion of the house being haunted too late to hear what had sparked it. He was about to explain when his mother yelled up from downstairs.

'Kids!'

'OK!' he called back. 'I'll show it to you when we get back,' he said to Damon. 'It was in that box of things your dad found down in the cellar.'

156

They trooped downstairs and followed their mother out to the car. By unspoken consent, Cassie got to sit in the passenger seat at the front. It was a bit of squash in the back with the other boys, but Joel didn't really mind.

'Can we go to the library after?' Cassie asked her mother as they drove.

'Whatever you want, honey.' Their mother nodded agreeably. She seemed both relieved and decidedly amazed that the four of them weren't trying to kill each other.

They passed most of the drive in silence, but a fairly agreeable one. His mother flicked the radio onto an oldies station, and that plus the motion of the car threatened to lull Joel into the sleep he'd missed the night before. When it was time to get out in the town, his legs had gone numb and he stumbled slightly on the pavement.

The air of the town somehow tasted different from that inside the house, and he was sure it was more than just a lack of dust and decay. He felt as though a lingering cold had finally left him or a weight had been lifted from his chest, and at last he could properly *breathe*.

The others seemed to notice the change too. Pale Tim appeared to get a little colour in his face, and straightened up instead of shrinking down into himself. When he wasn't half-cringing like he had been all the time in the house, he didn't look quite so young.

Joel's mother smiled fondly at them all as they tumbled out of the car. 'OK, people, what do we want to see? I heard that there's a ghost story just come out that's supposed to be—'

'No!'

'I don't think so.'

'No thanks, Mum.'

'— or maybe we could watch something else,' she completed dryly.

They ended up watching some kind of cartoon space adventure they were all too old for but enjoyed anyway. Cassie sat on the end next to Joel, but kept crawling over him to poke Damon in the arm and get the popcorn.

'Do I look like a settee?' he demanded irritably, the fourth or fifth time he got elbowed somewhere awkward.

'That'll teach you to wear leather.'

'It's only fake leather.'

'So are most settees.' She clambered back across Joel to sit down again.

Damon leaned over after her. 'Quiet at the end there. Some of us are trying to watch the movie.'

Cassie punched him in the shoulder, but it was the kind of playful blow she usually gave Joel.

After the film they got sandwiches in the café across the street. Damon dropped a cucumber slice down the back of Cassie's neck, and she retaliated by adding ketchup to his milkshake while he was in the toilet. He took a mouthful, winced, and then shrugged and drank the rest.

'Damon, that's gross,' Joel cringed.

He just grinned and patted his stomach. 'Hey, that stuff's mostly just sugar. And anyway, tomato's a fruit.'

'And you're a fruitcake,' Cassie told him, giving him a look.

Damon turned to their mother and batted his eyelashes. 'She thinks I'm sweet.'

'I was going more with thick, square and nutty,' she said archly, but spoiled it by laughing.

Joel glanced across at his mother, and caught her smiling quietly to herself.

When they had finished eating, she stood up and said, 'OK, kids, I've got some shopping to do. You guys want to go to the library and meet me outside the shop in an hour or so?'

Damon looked like he might be about to suggest a more interesting alternative, but Joel caught the swift movement of Cassie's elbow as she nudged him sharply. 'Could we, Mum?' she said quickly. 'I'd like to look at some books on the village. See if they've got anything on our house.'

'You know, Gerald cleaned up that box of papers from the cellar for you to have a look through,' their mother reminded her rather pointedly.

Joel saw Cassie's face darken momentarily, but she just said neutrally, 'Joel had a look last night. It's not the sort of stuff I want.'

Their mother looked irritated for an instant, but smoothed her face out with a little effort. 'Then we'll see if we can find you anything else,' she said.

'OK, what are we doing here?' Damon demanded when she'd dropped them off at the library.

Cassie rolled her eyes. 'Looking for a clue to who the ghost is, moron.'

'Like they're going to keep a list of everyone who died in the house, moron?' he shot back.

'This is why we're going to have to use a little thing called deduction – I'm not surprised you haven't heard of it; it involves using your brain.' She looked around. 'OK, we don't have much time, so I'll look through the newspaper archives, and Joel, you can see what they've got in the way of books on local history. You two – go and play with the blocks in the children's library or something.'

Damon did indeed wander off to do his own thing, but Tim stuck with Joel, investigating the stand of books and leaflets about the local area.

'What are we looking for exactly?' he wondered, as Joel opened up the most likely looking book, with a sepia photograph of the village pub on the front.

'I don't know. Anything about the house, I guess. I can't see that there'd be anything about who'd lived there, but if Sanderson built it himself, there might be something about him. Oh, and see if there's anything about a local family named Hawkins. I'm not sure if that was his wife's maiden name or her first husband, but if there's any stuff about the family it might mention her.'

'OK.'

There was silence for a while as they both flipped pages and read.

'The Sanderson house— Oh, nothing.' Tim cut himself off in the middle of his excited outburst. 'It just says he was a rich architect who came to the village to build his dream house.'

He put the book back and opened another. Joel had just found the right page in his own.

'Hey, listen to this! It's got more about him in this one. Apparently he was a bit stand-offish and snobby and most of the locals didn't like him. He hired a couple of people to do building work, but he was kind of obsessive about getting the details perfect.'

'My dad hates people like that,' Tim put in.

'They can't all have hated him, though. After all, he did marry a local girl . . . Yeah, see, it's in here. Victoria Hawkins, she married him after her brother did some carpentry work on the house.' He turned the page. 'Oh . . . but it didn't last long. They were only together for a few years before she had enough of his obsession with getting the house perfect and left him. And—' He froze, feeling suddenly chilled. 'It says he killed himself.'

They exchanged troubled glances. 'In the house?' Tim wondered hesitantly.

'It doesn't say.' Joel frowned. 'But still, it can't be *his* ghost, because the house wouldn't even have existed when he was a kid. And who's the other boy? It doesn't make sense.'

A call from Cassie broke into their mutual puzzlement. 'Hey, Joel! I found something.' They hurried over.

'Article on Sanderson.' She presented it. 'Apparently he committed suicide.'

'We just read that,' Joel told her.

'Oh. Well, anyway, look, he *did* have kids, because according to the article, it was his wife and children leaving him that made him finally go nuts. He fired everybody working for him, went mental finishing off all the work on the house at lunatic speed, and then he killed himself.'

Joel was shaking his head. 'Yeah, but they can't have been the boys from the photo, though. I was just reading – Victoria Hawkins was a local, he only met her during the years he was building the house. So if they had kids together, they would only have been babies when she left.'

Cassie frowned. 'So who is he, then, your mysterious ghost-boy? Some kid from whatever family moved in once the house fell vacant?'

'As long as it wasn't Sanderson's ghost that killed him,' Joel said darkly.

His sister sighed. 'Well, whatever happened to him, the newspapers aren't going to help. I looked through – this isn't a big place: you'd think a kid getting killed would be front page news.'

'Then there has to be something we've missed,' said Tim.

'Yeah . . .' said Joel slowly. They *had* missed something. Or rather, he thought, missed the significance of something. There was a nagging feeling at the back of his mind that there was some little fact he was forgetting, something he'd read or heard or seen somewhere that would shed light on it all . . .

Cassie broke his train of thought by standing up. 'There probably is – but we won't find it here. I know you don't like the idea, but the fact is, if this ghost is hanging around because he has unfinished business, then the only one who can tell us what we need to know is the ghost himself.'

As they headed out of the records section, Joel looked around. 'Where's Damon?'

'Probably looking for nude pictures in the art books.' Cassie rolled her eyes.

In fact, they found him in the children's department. Cassie snorted aloud as she saw the Dr Seuss book he was flicking through. 'Oh, found our level, have we?'

Damon just smiled slightly sadly at the pages. 'Wow, this brings back memories.'

'Of when you were even more immature than you are now?'

Ignoring her, he stretched out and slotted the book back into place. 'Remember when Mum used to read these to us, Tim? Before she got too sick?'

Tim shook his head slowly. 'I don't remember,' he said unhappily. Joel felt suddenly queasy, as if he was intruding on something very private. He'd been vaguely aware that the Wilder boys' mother had died several years ago, but neither of the boys had ever said anything about her.

Damon sighed heavily, and then clapped his brother on the shoulder. 'Come on, kid. Amanda's waiting for us.'

Joel and Cassie trailed after the Wilder boys, exchanging troubled glances. If the two of them thought it was bad replacing a dad who'd walked out without a backward glance when they were tiny, how much harder must it be to live with someone after your own parent had died? He tried to imagine what it would be like if something happened to Cassie and then his mother finally decided to adopt a new daughter to take her place. It made him feel pretty sick.

And poor Gerald. No wonder he always looked so

sad and distressed when the four of them weren't getting along.

Their mother picked up the sombre mood as they trooped out to join her by the supermarket. 'Everything all right, kids?' she asked with a frown.

'We're fine,' said Damon lightly. But he spent most of the journey back staring out of the car window into space, and even Cassie didn't try to tease him.

He came out of his dark mood as they approached the house, though, and hopped out of the car to help their mother with the shopping. 'Where do you want this, Amanda, in the kitchen?'

'Please,' she said gratefully, as Joel and Cassie scrambled to help with the rest of the bags.

Joel was steeling himself for the return of the unsettled feeling as he entered the house, but he was immediately distracted by the sound of banging and crashing coming from the cellar. It sounded like the kind of echoing metallic clangs you got when you accidentally kicked a radiator.

'God only knows what he's doing down there,' their mother observed, with a glance towards the stairs as she deposited her bags. Tim looked around the hallway nervously, as if worried the walls or ceiling might collapse at any moment.

'Maybe it'll drive the ghosts out,' Damon suggested brightly, when their mother was out of the room. 'They used to drive out evil spirits by banging and shouting and ringing bells.' He smirked at Cassie. 'I'm just full of useful information, aren't I?'

She gave him a look. 'Oh, is that what you're full of?' He sneered back, fairly playfully.

Joel followed his mother out to pick up the last of the bags. 'Hey, Mum,' he thought to ask as he accompanied her back to the car. 'Do you know anything about the people who used to live in this house? Cassie told me you said something about the guy who built it. I was just wondering how it ended up so beaten up. Why did it stay empty so long?'

'Well, I don't know that much,' she said with a shrug. 'Had an interesting conversation with one of the neighbours, though. Molly Sargent from the village – you remember me telling you about her? She had an aunt who used to live here when the place was first built.' She clicked her fingers. 'Oh, what was her name . . . ?'

'Victoria Hawkins?' Joel suggested tentatively.

'Hawkins!' she agreed triumphantly. 'Yes, that's right. She married the architect – not much of a love match, by all accounts. Apparently the honeymoon period was over pretty quick, and Victoria spent all the time she could with her sister-in-law: said she couldn't stand to be in the house a second longer than she had to.'

'Wow, that's a great recommendation,' Joel said rather bitterly. Of course – Mum and Gerald wouldn't have thought to pay any attention even if anyone *had* tried to warn them about this place.

His mother smiled and shook her head at him as she locked the car. 'Somehow I doubt it was anything about the building that chased her out, Joel. According to Molly, Mr Sanderson was much more interested in his dream of a perfect house than he was in his wife and children. It's no surprise that she eventually packed up and did a runner in the middle of the night – the only strange thing was that she didn't go back to her family in the village. Too embarrassed, probably, after she'd had a big fight with her brother over marrying the man in the first place.'

Too embarrassed – or too petrified, perhaps. Joel

could only imagine that if he had to endure months or years of the terrifying things that had been happening since they'd moved here, he'd be about ready to run away and never come back too.

Had this house been haunted since the very moment it was built? If so, what had made it that way? And who *were* those two boys? He still didn't understand what they had to do with any of this, and why their picture should have been in the box in the cellar.

'Who lived here after the Sandersons?' he asked. 'The house seems like it's been empty for decades.'

'Not quite, although it's true no one ever took up residence for very long,' she conceded. 'The trouble was that no one wanted to move in after Mr Sanderson died in the house – gave the place a bit of a bad reputation, I suppose. And it couldn't have been cheap when it was still new, a big place like this, so it stood empty for a good few years. That sort of thing starts a vicious circle: the house is in a bad state, so buyers can't deal with fixing it up, so it gets in a worse state, so people are even *less* interested . . .'

'Until we came along, and bought it anyway,' he concluded.

'Well, we always were crazy,' she said cheerfully.

Damon had already made a start on unpacking the shopping when they rejoined him in the kitchen. There was still a lot of crashing and banging coming from the cellar.

'What's going on down there?' Joel wondered.

He shrugged. 'I dread to think. Amanda, I've put all the cold and frozen stuff away.'

'Thank you very much, Damon.' She patted him on the shoulder in gratitude. 'Why don't you boys go and see what Gerald's up to down there? I can unpack the rest of this – I'm the only one who knows where everything goes at the moment.'

'OK. Thanks, Mum.'

The air in the basement was even staler than that in the rest of the house, and Joel coughed on his way down as he swallowed dust. Damon absently thumped him on the back. 'Ow,' he protested, grimacing.

'Shouldn't cough then, should you?'

They found Gerald, covered in grime, standing with his hands on his hips as he regarded the crumbling brick walls of the cellar.

'What're you doing, Dad?' Damon asked.

'Wrestling with the pipes – and doing some think-ing.' Gerald nodded at the back wall. 'D'you reckon the house'll fall down if I knock that out?'

Damon shrugged and looked up at the ceiling spec-ulatively. 'Maybe.'

'Shall I try it and find out?'

Joel coughed again. 'Why'd you want to take the wall out?' he wondered.

Gerald stretched out his arms to indicate the space. 'Look at this. This isn't a full-sized cellar, not for a house this big. Doesn't look like a patch job – all these walls are original – so I'm just wondering why they didn't extend it further that way.' He gestured towards the far wall. 'I want to see if there was some reason, or if they just couldn't be bothered digging out a bigger one.'

'Hence, knocking big holes in the wall?' Damon said.

'Well, a little hole would probably be a better idea,' Gerald said wryly. He ran a hand over the crumbling stonework. 'I should be able to knock a few of these bricks out quite easily, I think.'

'How?'

174

He pointed out an oversized hammer standing propped against the wall. 'With that.'

'That's real advanced technology there, Dad,' Damon said.

Gerald pulled an exaggeratedly macho pose. 'It's a struggle of nature! Man against the stonework.'

'Yeah, but think how embarrassing it'll be if you lose.'

Gerald grinned at Joel. 'You reckon you can lift that?' he asked.

He eyed the hammer gingerly. 'No,' he admitted honestly.

'You want to give it a try?'

Joel crossed the room and wrapped his hands around the handle, but the sheer weight of the thing defeated him. He managed to get it about a millimetre off the ground, and immediately dropped it with a loud clang.

'Let me try.' Damon shouldered him aside and hefted the hammer. With an effort, he succeeded in lifting it and even raising it a little way. Pride thus preserved, he put it down again with a grateful groan. 'So are you going to knock the wall in today?' he asked his father.

Gerald glanced up at the ceiling. 'It'd be a bit noisy, I think, somehow. And I still have to finish fixing the door. Best leave it for another day; there's no hurry.'

Damon gave him a knowing look. 'Ah – you can't lift the big hammer properly either.'

'Get out of here,' Gerald chided him affectionately, and the two boys scrambled back up the stairs.

'I'm all covered in dust now,' Joel observed, wiping his hands unhappily on his jeans.

'Hey, where's Tim?' Damon wondered.

'Maybe he's upstairs.'

They both trooped out of the kitchen to look for the others. Joel felt a brief shudder slide down his spine as they passed the doorway of the master bedroom, even though the door was closed. He quickly hurried on, leaping up the stairs and scrubbing his palms once again on his clothes before knocking on Cassie's door.

It wasn't properly closed, and swung open under his knuckles. 'Cass, have you seen—?'

He stopped abruptly as he registered the unlikely sight before him – his sister's chess set arranged mid-game on top of a box, and she and Tim sitting calmly to either side of it.

Cassie glared at his and Damon's incredulous expressions. 'What?' she demanded challengingly.

XVIII

Joel lounged on his belly on Cassie's bed, chin resting on one hand. Damon sat near his feet, with his long legs folded up to his chest.

'So what do we do now?' the older boy wondered, rubbing the back of his neck.

'We *have* to contact the ghost,' Cassie insisted, not taking her eyes off the chess board. She made a quick move, and Tim frowned in concentration.

Damon narrowed his eyes. 'Whoa there, crazy girl, didn't we try that before?'

'And we made contact.'

'And nearly got our heads blown off!'

'It wasn't trying to hurt us,' she insisted.

'Oh, and how do you know?' he demanded. 'Go, team Tim,' he added, as his younger brother took one of Cassie's knights.

'Bad idea.' She smirked as she swiped the castle he'd just taken it with. 'I don't think the ghost was trying to do anything to us – it just didn't realize its own strength. So the glass exploded – big whoop! I bet if *you* were trying to move something around with your mind, you'd be pretty clumsy too. You know, in theory, if you had an actual brain.' Damon just smiled nastily at her in response. 'It's a little boy ghost!' Cassie exclaimed, frustrated. 'What are you all so afraid of?'

'It's not the boy's ghost,' Joel said.

At the same time Tim said, 'Not *him*—'

They exchanged a glance. 'It's what's coming after him,' Joel finished.

Cassie paused, a white bishop caught between her fingers. 'What do you mean, what's after him?'

Joel struggled to put fleeting impressions into words. 'I . . . I dream. About this house. Ever since we got here.' Tim was nodding emphatically.

'There— Sometimes I'm up in the loft, in that cupboard where both me and Tim got trapped. And there's a little boy crouched down in there next to me, and he's—'

'—praying,' Tim completed.

'Yeah. The same words, over and over again.'

'*If I should die before I wake, I pray the Lord my soul to take*,' they chorused dully together, and Joel felt the echoes of his nightmare in it.

'And I know there's something – there's somebody *out there*, looking for us, but before they figure out where we're hiding, I wake up.'

'And there are other dreams,' Tim added solemnly.

'Running through the house, trying to get away—'

'And you know they're chasing but you can't look round—'

'And then out in the garden—'

'Trying to get over the fence—'

'Trying to get out into the village where you'll be safe, but just as you're about to get over—'

'A hand grabs you by the ankle,' Tim concluded. The two boys exchanged a wide-eyed look, and Joel felt his heart begin to pound harder in his chest as if he was back there in that garden, scrabbling to get out—

The older two were staring at them. 'No escape . . .' said Damon softly.

Cassie shook her head in confusion. 'I don't understand. You've both been having the same nightmares? How come it's only you two who've been dreaming all this stuff?'

Joel didn't have a clue, but Tim surprised him by speaking up. 'I think . . . there were two boys. And one of them was our age and the other one was younger. Something . . . something *happened*, something horrible happened to both of them, and now they're trapped here, haunting the house. And it's the older boy we've both been dreaming about.'

Joel slowly began to piece it together. 'The boys must have . . . they must have seen something, had some reason to be scared, and they tried to hide in the cupboard up there. But they were found, and—' He swallowed, not really wanting to think what might have happened to the boy who had been praying. 'And only the older one got away. Then he was chased right through the house, and he managed to get out into the garden, but then—' Joel broke off. He had to blink away a burning sensation from his eyes, as if he were close to tears. He didn't know anything about those two boys apart from the brief snatches he'd seen in his dreams, but the thought of what had happened to them . . .

And of course, he didn't *know* what had happened to them, and that somehow made it worse.

'Kids!' They all jumped at the bellow up the stairs. 'Can you stop running around up there? I can hear you right through the floor!'

'Sorry, Mum!' Joel yelled back automatically. He exchanged a glance with the other three – who were all sitting still, not so much as tapping their feet.

Cassie placed a finger to her lips in a 'shh' gesture. They all listened.

The pounding of rapid footsteps outside the room was suddenly clearly audible. With sweat trickling down the back of his neck, Joel heard them thunder across the landing and past Cassie's door. He didn't have to think for even a second to guess where they were going. There was a series of urgent crashes and thumps, and the muffled slam of a closing door.

'That was the cupboard,' Tim said quietly.

His sister was the first to stand, and Damon immediately followed her. They made their way towards the door with cautious footsteps, and Cassie twisted the handle painfully slowly to silence the sound of the latch. Damon took the edge of the door as she opened it, guiding it to a stop against the wall without banging.

Joel didn't want to follow, but was also reluctant to be left behind. Tim trailed at the rear, arms wrapped tightly across his stomach as if he was afraid he might fly apart into pieces if he let go of himself.

They all tilted their heads up at the same time. The hatch stood ajar; with a single touch of Cassie's fingertips, the ladder slid the rest of the way down and locked into place. It creaked faintly, uncomfortably like a soft and mournful sigh.

The four of them exchanged glances; no one wanted to be the first to go up. After a moment Damon took the lead.

The loft was empty. Despite their care in clearing up, Joel felt a shard of glass crunch under his elbow as he pulled himself up. Even as he registered what it was, it still made him jump.

The cupboard door was in shadow, but they could all see that it was closed. For a while nobody moved, and then Cassie started forward. Damon immediately overtook her, striding over to grasp the handle before she could reach it. Joel was abruptly reminded of the way he'd braced himself, straining to yank it open when Tim was trapped inside. Maybe Damon was too, because he set his jaw and tugged with much greater strength than the job needed.

The door flew open, and—

And nothing. It was just a cupboard. Empty of corpses, bloodstains, and indeed anything but cobwebs, shadows and splintered floorboards, and that piece of ancient graffiti on the wall. It looked just like any other part of this house: battered, and in need of a serious clean.

In the moment that followed, Tim let out a nervous giggle. At almost the same instant Joel felt a *whoosh* of motion past his ear, and the ladder bounced violently in position as if someone had thrown all their weight against it, descending at speed.

'Cassie! Joel!' came an exasperated shout from downstairs.

'Sorry, Mum, the ladder slipped out of my hand!'

They all exchanged glances – Cassie throwing in a quick glare at the Wilder boys because her mother hadn't included their names in the implied rebuke – and headed back down onto the landing. No sign of . . . anything.

'Do you think it's gone?' Tim asked tentatively.

'I don't know.' Joel peeked cautiously around the doorframe into Cassie's room: everything looked normal to him. 'I guess.' They hesitantly moved back in and took up their previous places – albeit in considerably less relaxed poses than before.

Damon shook his head as he sat back down. 'What was all that a—?'

'Our chess pieces have moved.' Tim regarded the board suspiciously.

Cassie frowned. 'Yeah. Hey, yeah! I was winning!'

Damon smirked. 'Guess the ghost doesn't like you either.'

'Shut up.' She looked around, and then up at the ceiling, as if wondering where to face to address the ghost. 'Hey, are you there? You want to play chess with me? You can—'

As if someone had taken an abrupt swipe at the side of it, box and chess set both went flying. Pieces scattered across the room, and Joel quickly trapped one with his palm before it escaped under the bed. A black knight rolled to a halt a couple of metres out in the hall.

'That's pretty much how I feel about chess,' Damon quipped shakily. They all scrambled to their feet. Tim was drawing deep breaths, as if he was having trouble getting them through his chest.

'You know what?' said Joel carefully.

'What?' asked Cassie, eyes still fixed on the chess explosion littering her bedroom floor.

'I think we should probably do the rest of our talking out in the garden.'

'Good idea.'

They fled the house.

Cassie lay stretched out on her stomach, absently twirling strands of long grass around her fingers as she spoke. 'I still say we should try to talk to it. Them. However many ghosts there are in there.'

'Oh yeah, because *that*'s been resoundingly success-ful so far,' Damon said sarcastically.

'Oh, come on. The ghost *wants* us to notice it, or why do all this stuff? Think about it. It kicked over the chess set. So imagine you saw me do that. Why would you think I'd done it?'

'Because you're a scary crazy evil girl?'

She narrowed her eyes at him. 'Because I was frustrated – say, just for example, at being trapped in a house with some spectacularly dense, annoying, immature—'

Joel decided it probably wouldn't hurt to interrupt that before it ended up somewhere that would get them all in trouble. 'You think the ghost is trapped?'

'It said there was no escape,' she reminded him.

'Unless it meant no escape for *us*,' said Tim grimly, looking pale.

Damon gave him a light punch of encouragement on the shoulder. 'Chill out, little guy. It hasn't killed us yet, has it?'

'Exactly!' Cassie pounced. 'Come on! It blew up a glass, threw stuff all over the place, ripped up those plastic sacks – if it wanted to do us some serious damage, it could.'

Tim winced, and Damon shot her an irritated glare over his brother's shoulder. 'Thanks, Cassie.' He scowled.

She shrugged, and smiled sharply. 'Any time.' She looked across at Joel. 'Listen, I don't know what's happening with these dreams you're having, but I'm telling you, this ghost is *not* trying to hurt us. It could if it wanted to; it hasn't.'

'Yet,' Tim pointed out tremulously.

She whipped round as if she was about to snap at him, but stopped herself and just rolled her eyes. 'Yeah, OK, yet. But what's it waiting for, Christmas?'

Damon frowned, resting his chin on a clenched fist. 'Psycho-girl has a point,' he noted mildly.

Cassie gave him a smile that was mostly a baring of her teeth. 'Thank you for your support, fruitcake boy.'

He smirked coolly back. 'Thank you for acknowledging that support—'

Joel jumped in quickly before another round of name-calling could begin, even in the current relatively playful fashion. 'Um, can we . . . ?' He gestured vaguely, not really indicating anything except his desire to get back to more useful topics.

'Yeah.' Damon breathed out, and ran a hand through his fine dark hair. 'OK, so the question is . . . what now?'

Cassie tapped a foot thoughtfully on the grass. 'I think we should try another séance.'

They all rounded on her in disbelief. '*Cassie*—'

'Come *on*—'

'I don't think we—'

'Listen to me!' she roared abruptly, shutting them all up. She smiled at their silence, and calmly smoothed out the fabric of her shirt. 'Thank you. Listen. I think that when we were up in the loft, we were too close to the source. It was too powerful. The ghost was trying to speak to us at first; it was trying to give us a message, but I think—' Her forehead and nose wrinkled up, as they always did when she was concentrating deeply, and she broke off for a moment.

Damon smirked again. 'You actually think? Because so far, there hasn't been that much evidence of—'

'Shut *up*, Damon.' She rolled her eyes, but was too far away to manage much more than an indignant prod to his belly. 'I *think*,' she repeated, glaring, 'that when the ghost was trying to talk to us, it got caught up in the . . . the echo up there.'

'Echo?' Joel frowned, but Tim seemed to have got it.

'You mean it was . . .' He screwed his face up in contemplation. 'Like the dreams we've been having. The ghost might not even be *trying* to put them in our heads, but those memories . . . the echoes of those things that happened here are too strong to die away.'

'Exactly!' Cassie pointed and snapped her fingers at him. She glanced across at Joel. 'That . . . chant thingy, the "If I should die" – that was from your dreams, wasn't it?' He and Tim nodded in mute agreement, and Joel once again felt the flesh of his arms crawl up into goosebumps.

If I should die before I wake, I pray the Lord my soul to take. If I should die before I—

'Yeah.' His voice sounded ragged to his own ears, and he swallowed briefly. 'Yeah,' he repeated. Tim shot him a sympathetic glance.

Cassie nodded slowly to herself, as if confirming a theory. 'I don't really know how ghosts . . . work, or anything, but it seems to me like if the whole of this house is haunted, parts of it are . . . *more* haunted, you know? The parts where . . . whatever it is . . . is strongest.'

Joel was nodding mechanically along with the words as she spoke, his head feeling like it was only loosely attached to his body as it flopped up and down. A cloud had passed over the sun, and the previously bright afternoon now seemed greyer and colder.

'I think the cupboard is so haunted that it's left kind of a – an imprint, you know?' his sister continued. 'And it's so strong that when we were trying to get the spirit to just speak to us, the echoes up there were too loud for us to hear it. Like . . . well, you know how on that crappy TV your dad's got set up in the lounge—'

'*Hey*—' Damon began to retort, scowling, but Cassie rode straight on over him.

'You sometimes get, like, two different channels at the same time, bleeding into each other? Or – radio stations!' she said triumphantly. 'Where you're trying to tune into this really faint signal, and then *wham!* Radio Four or something cuts in really strong and totally drowns it out.'

'You think we were running our little two-way radio setup, and we suddenly got an earful of Radio Dead Guy?' Damon asked.

It was easy for him to be flip about it, Joel thought. He didn't understand the horror that tuning into that terrible flat monotone really meant.

If I should die before I wake— Even out here in the garden, the choking desperation of being utterly trapped descended on him like a blanket soaked in ice-water. Maybe Cassie was right, and that echo, that imprint of a terrible, terrible thing had flooded out what they were trying to do. As fully as it flooded out his thoughts, blanking everything but the endless repetition of that horrifying, toneless chant.

– my soul to take. If I should die before I wake, I pray the Lord my soul to take. If I should—

Joel gasped, his breath coming out in a sudden burst, and Cassie and Damon both looked at him oddly for a moment. Then his sister leaned forward, placing a hand flat in the long grass between them.

'We need to do another séance— Wait, J,' she cut him off as he moved to protest. 'Not up in the loft – that's obviously too close to the source of the haunting. Downstairs, I guess, somewhere where there's plenty of space and we won't get trapped.'

Joel was pretty sure the ghost could trap them just

about anywhere it felt like, no matter how many doors there were, but before he could try and force out a protest through the numbness of anxiety, Damon spoke up.

'Oh, yeah, sure, Dad and Amanda are going to love that. Shall we tell them it's the latest schoolyard craze, or invite them to sit in?'

Cassie gave him her best 'duh' look. 'We'll wait till they go out again, *moron*.' There were nastier things she could have called him, but she loaded that one word with more than enough venom to make up for it.

Damon sneered right back. 'Oh, and how d'you know they're even going to—?'

'Bet you a tenner they do.'

He narrowed his eyes at her. 'You don't even have any money.'

'No, but I will have very soon.'

'Hey! You want cash, get a freakin' paper round. I'm not your personal—'

'Kids!' Their mother's bellow from the back step interrupted them. 'Can you come in please?'

They dutifully traipsed back inside, brushing dead

summer grass from their clothes. Their mother gave them a quick smile, turned lopsided as she put her earrings in. Joel noticed she had her favourite silver blouse on.

'Gerry and I are going out to dinner,' she explained. She shot a wary glance at Cassie as she spoke, but Cassie was busy shooting a smug look Damon's way. 'There's chips in the oven, and if you want to microwave some mini pizzas or something—'

'Sure, no problem, I can sort it out,' Damon offered with a shrug, and she smiled at him.

'Thank you, Damon.' She turned to look at the rest of them. 'We shouldn't be that late – we'll be back before half ten unless we get lost somewhere.' She gave Joel and Cassie a stern look. 'You'll get yourselves to bed if we're any later than that?' It might be phrased as a question, but they knew an order when they heard it.

'Yes, Mum.'

'OK.'

She seemed satisfied with their promises. True enough, ordinarily they'd keep to them – well, close enough, anyway – but somehow Joel doubted that he'd be in bed tonight one second earlier than he absolutely had to. One way or another.

His mother leaned against the wall as she stood on one leg to adjust her heels. 'OK. I'll give you a shout when we leave.'

'OK, Mum.'

'Bye, Amanda.'

'All right.' She cast around the kitchen vaguely, as if trying to figure out what else she'd forgotten to do. 'Pizzas are in the freezer – you'll have to fight it out over who gets what,' she added on her way out of the room.

'I call ham and pineapple,' Cassie burst out instantly. She looked at Damon. 'And I believe you owe me a tenner?'

'I didn't take that bet!' he reminded her as he ducked into the next room to open the freezer.

Joel nudged his sister. 'So, you're psychic now?'

'Mum told me earlier,' she grinned. She seemed to have forgotten all about making her usual grimaces of disgust at the idea of Mum and Gerald going out together. 'Listen, it'll be perfect. We'll have the house to ourselves for hours – plenty of time to hold another séance without them walking in on us. And we'll do a proper one this time. No fooling around.'

Joel frowned. 'Cassie, I'm not sure—'

'We've got to do it, Joel,' she said seriously. 'We can't just sit around waiting for more and more things to happen. And this is the only way we stand a chance of finding out the truth.' She turned to follow Damon. 'Grab the pizza cutter, would you?'

Knowing he couldn't argue with her, he said nothing, and fumbled in the kitchen drawer. For a moment, as he pulled it out, the pizza cutter seemed to glint in the light and take the shape of a blood-stained knife.

Dinner that evening was a tense meal, but not in the usual way. Joel could feel the weight of sick anticipation lurking deep down in his stomach, leaving little room for slightly singed pizza on top of it. Tim too was picking at his food, but Cassie seemed unconcerned and Damon ate like somebody might snatch his plate away if he didn't finish fast enough.

Joel couldn't help thinking that his sister and Damon just . . . didn't get it. Oh, they'd seen the ghost at work, they knew it was real now, but still . . .

To them, this was cool. A real live – well, dead –

ghost, throwing things around; a mystery to be solved, or at least marvelled over. They could see the evidence of the ghost's presence, but they didn't *feel* it, at least not in the way he and Tim did.

Maybe it was just that they were older; they didn't have that same immediate connection with the ghost of a boy who'd died when he was only just coming up to Joel's age. Or perhaps it was as much to do with their personalities – both Cassie and Damon were loud and self-assured and not afraid to stand up and shout whatever they were thinking. Maybe it was harder for a ghost to reach out and touch some-body like that; somebody who lived their life on the outside instead of wrapped up in their own head, in their thoughts and imagination.

Whatever the reason, he and Tim seemed to be the only ones who were really tuned into the suffo-cating atmosphere inside the house. The others might witness moving objects and exploding glassware, but they weren't having the dreams, and he didn't think they had any real idea of the stomach-wrenching horror underlying it all. They saw, but they didn't feel – at least, not nearly on the same level.

As he scraped the last few uneaten chips into the bin by the back door, Joel looked out of the window. The sky was overcast, giving the impression that it was night already. All he could see in the glass was his own reflection, shadows turning his eyes into dark hollows. It gave him the unpleasant sensation of being face to face with his own skull.

He found Cassie crouched in a corner of the dining room, going through some of the bags they hadn't got around to unpacking yet. 'What are you looking for?'

She didn't look up. 'I figure that if we're going to do this again, it's stupid to have all the letters written out on paper like before,' she explained. 'They just flew everywhere, and I don't think we want to try using a glass again – it's amazing none of us got cut to pieces. Shatterproof, my— Ah-ha!' She'd obviously found what she was looking for, and proceeded to retrieve it with much rustling and tugging.

'It would be easier if you lifted the boxes out, you know,' he observed.

'Quiet, you.' She finally produced a clear bag

full of plastic squares and waved it triumphantly.

Despite everything, he had to smile. 'Scrabble letters?'

'Well, I figured that the ghost can just move these around, and that way we won't have to worry about broken glass or the letters getting blown away.' Cassie rummaged through the bag, and frowned. 'I don't think we ever found that missing Q. Do you think it's going to need to spell anything with a Q in it?' She seemed to be genuinely troubled by this possibility – more so than by the idea of trying to make contact with the restless dead.

'Cassie, I really don't think—'

'Course it'll work,' she cut him off, not waiting to find out that he hadn't been intending to make that particular protest in any case. He had no trouble believing this was going to *work*. 'Get Tim and Damon,' she ordered. 'Mum and Gerald shouldn't be back for a few hours, but they might be early.'

She acted as if it had never occurred to her that he might protest, and somehow that made it impossible to do so. He delayed the inevitable for as long as possible by ducking into the bathroom before he went upstairs. It was probably a smart idea to have an empty bladder, anyway.

Nothing moved in the murky glass of the mirror as he smudged sweat from his forehead with a towel, but he didn't find that remotely reassuring. It was the calm before the storm. Or rather, the calm before his sister marched on in and kicked up a storm.

Why were they doing this? He should just refuse, right here, right now, and tell them it was crazy. Tim would back him up. Tim would understand.

Except . . .

Except, what if they *didn't* do this? What was the alternative? Carry on living in a house where every shadow could hold a hidden menace, where he almost didn't dare go to sleep because of the horrific images that were sure to invade his dreams?

Mum and Gerald had practically bankrupted themselves to move into this house; it wasn't like they were going anywhere anytime soon. And he somehow doubted that they'd listen to their kids if they insisted it was haunted, no matter how hysterical they got over it. The ghost had never done anything in front of either of the adults. Either they weren't receptive to it, or it was too wary of them to show itself.

For the first time since the cloud of fear had descended to fog up his thoughts, Joel stopped to consider what Cassie had been demanding to know all along. What did the ghost *want*?

He remembered its message. *Escape. No escape.* At first he'd thought that was a dire warning to the four of them, but when he thought of the dreams – the cupboard, running through the garden, a hand coming out of nowhere to grab him by the ankle – maybe it was the *ghost* that couldn't escape.

But why not? Something terrible had happened here, that much he was certain of – but why hadn't the unfortunate spirit been freed by death? What was binding it to this place, forcing it to stay, forcing it to endlessly return to those horrific final events?

If I should die before I wake, I pray the Lord my soul to take. If I should die before I wake, I pray the Lord—

'Joel!'

He jumped, even as his brain translated the bellow into his sister's voice. 'Sorry!' he yelled automatically.

He realized he was still standing staring blankly into the bathroom mirror, towel in hand. He threw it across the rack and unlocked the door.

'Sorry,' he repeated, as Cassie pulled an exasperated face at him.

'What were you doing in there? Learning to swim?'

'I was just . . .' He shrugged, but she wasn't really paying attention to his answer anyway.

'Come on.' She grabbed him by the arm and yanked him upstairs. Every creak of the steps underfoot sounded like a gunshot.

Damon met them at the top of the stairs. He looked tense, and Joel noticed he'd pulled on a thick, chunky sweater over his clothes. So did Cassie; she raised an amused eyebrow. 'Fashion statement?'

'I was cold,' he explained shortly, tugging at the material to loosen it about his shoulders. Joel could feel the hairs on his own arms and the back of his neck stand to attention, but he didn't think it was anything to do with the temperature. At least, not any natural temperature. It felt like they were inside an ice box, and if he was to go downstairs and open the door he would find the outside world was ten times warmer. He glanced towards the window over the stairs, and saw that the sky was full of purple-grey thunderheads, as if a storm was brewing.

Joel breathed out slowly, and was almost surprised when he didn't see a puff of pale breath like on any winter morning. Tim padded out to join them word-lessly, and they all flinched at the movement, even Cassie.

'Where are we going to do this? The hall?' Damon asked.

'No, that's—'

'No.'

He and Tim spoke together. 'The hall's out,' Joel continued alone. 'The master bedroom – that's another place like the loft.'

'It's too exposed, anyway,' Cassie said firmly. 'There's the front door – and we can't block the stairs.'

'Against what?' Damon wanted to know.

Cassie only shrugged. 'The front room,' she decided. 'It's got two doors, there are dustsheets we can use to cover the floor, and we can move the stuff out. We don't want anything loose left in there to fly around.' Joel no longer needed to ask if his sister was taking things seriously. This tense, low-voiced discussion bore more resemblance to a battle plan than to any kind of game.

'This is going to get rough, isn't it?' he said quietly. It wasn't really a question.

Tim smiled softly at him, but didn't speak. Cassie squeezed his arm briefly, and looked around at all of them, her usual cheerfully mocking smirk fading into gravity. It was Damon her eyes settled on last, as if she was finally admitting that he had at least as much a right to a voice as she did. 'Are we doing this?' she asked quietly.

His grey eyes were as serious as her brown ones as he slowly nodded. 'We're doing this.'

XXI

They filed into the front room like a funeral procession. Joel's eyes flew automatically to the wall where he'd seen the image of the ghost-boy earlier that morning. The only shadows cast there now were those of the TV on its makeshift stand, and ripples made by the billowing curtains. He walked over to close the big windows, requiring several sharp thumps with the heel of his hand to get the stiff catches moving.

'Dad's going to oil those soon,' Damon observed vaguely as Joel wandered back. All of them were drifting somewhat, unwilling to settle down, because that would mean having to go ahead and do this.

As usual, Cassie was the one to take charge. 'Joel, kick that dustsheet over here. We should spread it out on the floor in case the stuff gets thrown around again or something. We don't want to lose all these Scrabble tiles down the gaps in the floorboards.' She frowned in concern. 'We need to get that TV out of here—'

'I'll do it.' Damon moved over and hefted it with a grimace of effort.

'Oh, go on, Muscles,' Cassie said sarcastically. But she held the hall door open for him as he carried it out.

When they'd spread out the dustsheet, Tim sat down on it next to Joel, crossing his legs in a habit doubtless learned from school assemblies. 'This could be a very bad idea,' he said quietly.

'I know,' Joel agreed, just as softly. 'But what choice do we have?' They both kept their mouths shut as the other two came back to join them. Cassie dumped the Scrabble letters onto the middle of the sheet and started to sort them.

'Where's the Q?' Damon wondered.

She shot him a dark look. 'We haven't got one. We'll have to do without it.'

'Well, OK, but don't blame me if the ghost starts telling us to move "uickly".'

'Or to be "uiet",' Tim put in nervously.

Damon gave him a comforting smile across the circle. Really more of a square with just the four of them, Joel supposed, and a lopsided one at that. Despite having twice the space they'd had in the loft, they were crammed in as closely together as they could possibly be without knocking elbows.

'There's a blank tile! It'll cope!' Cassie snapped irritably. 'It seems to be intelligent, I know *I'm* intelligent – we'll just have to work around the rest of you. If it wants to tell us something vitally important, I don't think the lack of a Q is going to hurt too much.'

The boys lapsed into silence after that, and sat almost mesmerized as they watched Cassie's quick fingers separate and straighten out the letters. To Joel the room felt both too big *and* too small: the empty space behind his back was wide and threatening, but this tight little circle of the four of them was close and cramped, filled with the sound of their breathing.

'Well . . .' Cassie began and trailed off: the tiles were all arranged in a circle, and there was no more opportunity for time-wasting.

'What now?' Damon wondered.

'What . . . we did before, I guess?' Tim ventured tentatively.

'Except we're not using a glass,' his brother pointed out. Before, the act of reaching out to rest their finger-tips on the tumbler had at least provided some kind of focus.

'Should we hold hands?' Cassie wondered, look-ing somewhat disenchanted with this possibility.

Damon leaned sideways towards her and raised his eyebrows. 'Unable to resist my incredible allure?'

She gave him her most dazzling smile, and said, deceptively mildly, 'Would you like to try a whole new version of eating your words?'

'I think we should,' Joel said, stomach rolling with nerves. 'Uh, hold hands,' he added quickly, when everyone looked at him. 'Not feed Damon plastic tiles.'

'Can't we do both?' Cassie wondered. But she reached out to take her little brother's hand, and accepted Damon's with little more than a token grimace of distaste. Joel half imagined he could feel something surge through him as the four of them linked hands. But maybe that was just his stomach churning as dinner threatened to make a reappearance.

Tim's hand shifted sweatily in his.

'Ready?' Cassie asked softly.

'Ready,' Damon agreed.

'I guess,' said Joel tentatively. Tim just managed a single, anxious nod. He looked sickly pale; Joel didn't imagine he himself was looking any better.

His sister squeezed her eyes closed for a moment, and then tilted her head back as she'd done before. This time, however, she spoke plainly and simply. 'Are you there?'

Nothing.

Cassie hesitated for a long moment, and everything around them was so silent Joel clearly heard her as she swallowed before she spoke again. 'If you're there, use the letters. Talk to us. Tell us what you want.'

They all watched the collection of plastic tiles. Nothing moved. In fact, it was so still, Joel began to feel like all the air must have been sucked out of the room, and they were just sitting there, trapped in timeless nothingness. The air and his skin were both icy cold, but beads of sweat nonetheless began crawling down his back and across his forehead.

The fingers of his left hand were going numb where Cassie had them in a death grip. She'd always been able to crunch his bones like a pro when they were arm-wrestling, but he didn't think she knew she was doing it now. 'Talk to us,' she urged again, with quiet force.

Joel looked down, and saw the letter E nearest Cassie beginning to quiver. He didn't say anything, but perhaps he stiffened or made some quiet sound, for the others all followed his gaze.

He wasn't entirely surprised when the letters began to line themselves up into a familiar word. *Escape.*

'Ghost moves first, ten-point score,' said Damon softly, with a tremulous smile. Two more letters slid into place before the others.

No escape. Joel tensed, remembering how it had all gone horribly wrong after this point up in the attic.

'No escape for who?' his sister asked, tossing her head oddly; Joel recognized the gesture as a substitute for her usual nervous habit of flicking back her hair. She couldn't do that with her hands tightly closed around his and Damon's, but none of them dared to let go. 'For you?'

'You're trapped, aren't you?' All of them were surprised when Tim spoke up, licking his lips anxiously.

Joel flinched as the first half of the message was shunted aside almost angrily. Other letters fell in around the final three to form a new word. *Trapped*, the ghost told them, apparently agreeing.

'Why . . . why are you trapped here?' Joel asked hoarsely.

In front of him on the dustsheet, a new word formed. Just three letters: H − I − M. *Him*. They exchanged startled glances.

'Him . . . who?' Damon asked tentatively.

They all jumped as the three letters seemed to bounce a little way into the air and then fall back again. Joel imagined a frustrated fist, slamming hard against the wooden floor. *Him!*

'Who is he?' Cassie asked almost pleadingly. 'Can you tell us who he is? Can you tell us why he's keeping you trapped?'

A single plastic square slid out from amongst the others, and slowly came to rest by her hand. They all waited tensely, but nothing else moved. After a moment Damon very carefully extricated his hand from Cassie's and reached out to turn over the tile.

Both sides were blank.

C assie frowned in puzzlement. 'The blank tile?'

'Nil points for that,' Damon joked quietly, nervous. After a moment he retook Cassie's hand.

She hesitated before speaking again. 'We don't . . . I'm sorry, I don't . . . we can't understand. Blank – you don't know? Or . . . you can't tell us?'

The blank tile suddenly shot across the room and *pinged* off the doorframe. The rapid movement made Joel flinch, but at the same time it actually helped ease the terror building in his chest. A violent action, but it was one that he could understand; one that made sense to him. The ghost was frustrated, flailing around, like Cassie and her pointless anger at the Wilders' intrusion into their lives. Maybe it really *didn't* mean them any harm. Except . . .

Why are you trapped here? Him.

The ghost maybe couldn't – or wouldn't – tell them who 'he' was, but on some level Joel thought he knew.

Running through the house, trying to escape, trying to get over that fence but there's a hand on your ankle, and you know who it is, you know who it is, except it can't be, because what he did, what he did to—

It was there, almost, not quite a name but the sense of a person – like a word on the tip of his tongue, a feeling it would come to him if he only drove himself to try a little harder. He felt as if the ghost was . . . overlapping him, somehow, trying to force itself into the same space he occupied, trying to make him see what it had seen and know what it had known.

Just as it had been doing to Tim. The two younger boys, closest to the ghost, easiest for it to reach out and touch, were being pushed into reliving what must have been the last traumatic moments of its life. Perhaps being forced into seeing something that the ghost was unable to tell them in any other way.

Maybe, he realized slowly, it had been trying to communicate with them all along. Just not through anything so coolly distant as Cassie's hastily scraped-together séance ideas.

'Do you—?' His tongue felt thick in his mouth, and it was difficult to force the question out. 'Is there some way we can help you? Is there something we can do to—?'

They all yelled in shock as the pool of tiles exploded across the room, scattering in all directions and peppering them with squares of plastic. Joel instinctively let go of the others' hands to shield his face.

When the flurry of pings and thumps finally came to an end, he cautiously lowered his arms. A letter K had wound up in the fold of the right knee of his jeans, and he flicked it away with a shaky hand. Looking down, he saw that not all the letters had been angrily blasted away. A single, familiar message remained.

No escape.

Once again there was a brittle, fragile stillness. He

looked across at the others. Damon was massaging his forehead – one of the flying tiles must have struck him, unless it was a pressure headache from the atmosphere building in the room. Tim had his head down, and was breathing heavily through his mouth – whether to ward off sickness or rising panic, Joel couldn't guess.

Cassie's teeth were gritted in frustration, and her hands were balled into fists so tight they would surely leave nail marks in her palms. 'This isn't *working*,' she hissed. And though Joel thought it was working entirely too well, he understood exactly what she meant. They weren't getting *through*. They could communicate, but they couldn't ask the right questions, or the ghost couldn't give them an answer . . .

Without knowing why, he found himself getting to his feet. 'Please,' he said, although he wasn't even certain what he was pleading for until the rest of the words seemed to crowd their way into his mouth. 'We – we're trying to help you, we know you're trapped—'

Crunched down in the bottom of the closet, trying not to breathe, trying to hush your brother but you don't dare keep

222

your hand over his mouth because what if he starts struggling? And he won't stop chanting that old bedtime prayer because it's the only one he knows, and it doesn't even sound like a prayer any more, it sounds like an invocation for the dead—

If I should die before I wake, I pray the Lord my soul to take. If I should die before I wake—

Joel realized he was silently mouthing the words, and forced himself to stop.

'We know you're trapped,' he repeated thickly. He struggled to pull together brief flashes of vision and half-remembered nightmares. 'I know . . . you were hiding up in the loft. You and your little brother . . .' The ancient graffiti up in the loft drifted into memory, a young boy's carefully shaped letters. 'You and Michael. You were hiding because of . . . something you saw . . .'

He grasped at it, but the thought was too slippery, something he had only glimpsed from the corner of his mind's eye, the part of the story that was too horrific even to make it into nightmare.

Blood. Blood everywhere, and the knife—

His voice faltered, but then Tim was standing up beside him; he leaned heavily on Joel's arm to pull himself up, but his voice was surprisingly strong. 'You found her, didn't you?' Tim's face was screwed up in sweaty concentration, and Joel knew he was fighting through that same feeling of almost knowing. 'You saw what . . . he . . . did to your mother.'

The second Tim spoke it snapped into place in Joel's mind, not as something newly learned but rather as something he had already known, suddenly exposed. This was a part he hadn't seen, a part that Tim had been better able to grasp while his own mind shied away from it.

Yes. Not just blood, but a person, a death, a murder. A woman who had died in the same room as his mother slept in now, could have been the same age as her, lived nearly the same life. The part of the nightmare that he hadn't allowed himself to see, his mind deliberately cutting away to make it something not quite so final, something not quite so real.

But it was real, and it was terrible, and it had happened. And those two boys, crushed down in the bottom of that closet, trying desperately to keep quiet and still, had been *people*, not just whispered voices in the dark.

Joel saw it clearly, not in the visions of his nightmares but in the somehow even more horrifying eye
of his imagination. The two boys had come into the
house and they'd seen . . . whatever had happened
to their mother . . . and they'd run upstairs to hide.
Michael had been thrown into a loop by shock,
repeating the same line of prayer over and over until
it became meaningless, while his brother had just
desperately been trying not to make a sound . . .

But it hadn't worked.

'He found you,' Joel said, feeling as if he was hearing his own voice from a distance. Damon and Cassie
were both still sitting on the ground, looking up at him
and Tim with near-identical expressions of wide-eyed
confusion. At another time he might have found it
funny. Right now he was barely even seeing it. 'You
were hiding in there, and he opened the door and—'
He closed his eyes, breaking off, but Tim was on the
same wavelength.

'He got Michael, you couldn't help Michael, but
you tried to get away—'

Joel was there, running through the house, running
through the garden, living it himself.

'You got out into the garden, he was chasing you, but you were just trying to get over the fence, get to help, but—' This time Tim didn't fill the silence, and for a beat it hung there, unsaid. He slowly opened his eyes. 'But you didn't get away.'

And after that, nobody spoke at all. The silence hung solidly, like a blanket dropped over the room. Finally, it was shattered as a peal of thunder sounded outside, rumbling onwards and onwards until it seemed the very earth must be grinding itself apart.

The storm was breaking.

XXIII

Damon was the first to make a sound, a half-choked nervous chuckle. 'Thunder rolled,' he intoned, as if he was giving the stage directions for a play. 'Isn't that a little—?'

He was cut off by another bone-juddering peal, coming on suddenly enough to make Tim flinch. A blinding flash of lightning signalled that a third would be on its way at any moment. Despite the closed windows, the curtains billowed inwards.

'I don't think this is just a storm,' Joel said softly. He moved towards the window, but all he could see as he tugged aside the corner of the curtain was darkness and thick globules of rain splattering against the glass.

'Think your ghosts can control the weather, J?' his sister asked, but if she was aiming for sarcasm, it came out too close to a genuine question.

'Yeah, that's a bit— Don't you think that's pretty . . . ?' Damon trailed off.

Joel didn't know, but given that inside the house the temperature and pressure seemed to zigzag up and down with the mood of the ghosts . . .

'I think . . . we should get back from the window,' he said abruptly, more thunder threatening to obliterate the last of his words.

'What?' Cassie demanded, but Damon was already manhandling her back towards the doors, picking up something from Joel's tone of voice.

'Cass, I think you should probably—'

She struggled against his grip on her elbows, resistant to being shoved around just on general principle. 'Hey, get off me, you—'

Joel scrambled away from the far wall, pulling at Tim in passing, just as the window exploded inwards. Shards of glass rained down and scattered across the floorboards, and he was sure that if it hadn't been for the shielding of the thick curtains, they would both have been lacerated. As it was a fragment stung the back of his hand, and he swore more in startlement than in pain. The end of the dustsheet rose up in the strong wind, tangling itself around his legs.

Cassie froze in position. 'Uh . . . OK,' she said quickly, and stopped trying to resist being pulled.

They all scrambled out into the front hall, Tim grabbing Joel by the wrist to look at the back of his hand. 'Are you all right?'

'Yeah, it's just a nick,' he said quickly, yanking his arm away. It throbbed like a deep paper cut, but he didn't have time to care about it now.

Damon pulled his sweater closer about him in the sudden influx of moist, cold air, glancing warily around the room. 'Should we try to get outside?'

Joel shook his head. 'I don't think so.' As if in answer, the front door suddenly blew inwards, thumping so hard against the wall he was surprised it didn't jolt right off its hinges. A moment later the porch windows beside it shattered, one by one. Rainwater flooded in, spilling across the floor tiles and swirling aside long years' worth of dust.

'Then *where*?' Cassie demanded urgently.

'Not upstairs,' Tim insisted nervously. There was a sharp *ping* and a shower of glass and sparks as the light bulb overhead shattered, plunging the hall into semi-darkness. Joel looked around wildly. All the doors – front room, bathroom, even the glass door onto the porch – were rattling violently in their frames . . . except one. His mother's room.

His stomach dropped into his shoes. No. Not in there. They couldn't go in there . . .

'Come on!' Damon led the charge where Joel's feet refused to take him, running for the seeming refuge of the master bedroom. He seized the door handle; for a moment his muscles strained, and Joel was thrown into uneasy memories of the first time they'd been stuck up in the loft. Then, as abruptly as if somebody had let go of the handle on the other side – and wasn't *that* a happy thought? – it released.

A blast of ancient, dry and musty air seemed to hit Joel in the face, wiping out the earthy smell of the rain from outside and making him gag. He wanted to blurt out that this wasn't a good idea at all, but Damon either didn't feel or didn't care, and before he could find his voice he was hustled inside. He glanced back, and caught a glimpse of Tim's wide, frightened eyes before the door fell shut behind them, and everything was dark.

And still. Almost shockingly still, after the raging whorl of elemental anger that had been set loose in the other rooms. But it didn't feel like a safe haven – in fact, it felt a hundred times more threatening. Joel's breath was ragged in his throat, and he could hear his own heartbeat, too loud and much too fast.

They all jumped at a loud click, and the blaze of yellow light that followed. Damon smiled guiltily as he pulled his hand back from the switch and looked warily up at the bulb. It didn't explode; Joel supposed he should have found that reassuring. Somehow, he didn't.

Tim edged closer, and Joel made no sound of protest when the other boy's hand closed tightly around his wrist. Right now, any kind of human contact felt good.

Especially when you thought of all the *other* things

that might reach out and grab you by the wrist . . .

He shuddered, and Cassie gave him a tight smile. 'Stay cool, Joel,' she advised. 'We're safe from the storm in here, right?' Meant as a reassurance, it turned into a question. After all, he and Tim were the ones who felt things. And he felt . . .

Death. The musty stillness gave this room, with its brightly painted furniture and floral bedspread, an atmosphere like nothing so much as the inside of a tomb. A tomb where all the dead things weren't resting in anything resembling peace.

Tim's grip on his arm tightened so much it hurt, but that was almost welcome. Joel knew his tension must show in his face, and his sister looked at him worriedly.

'J . . .' She trailed off, because 'what's wrong?' was a pretty stupid question, when you got right down to it.

Damon tilted his head. 'It's gone quiet,' he observed softly. He was right; the crashing and banging and even the throaty rumble of the thunder had cut off completely. As if the silence in this room was a pool of dark liquid, spreading out to soak into everything around it and choke off every trace of sound.

'Don't open the door,' Cassie warned him.

'I wasn't going to!' Damon said with feeling.

What was wrong with them? thought Joel. Couldn't they feel it — couldn't they *feel* it? Tim made a softly strangled sound.

'It's OK, Tim,' Cassie said, and she touched his shoulder surprisingly gently.

But Joel shook his head. 'It's not.' Moving like a clockwork soldier, limbs travelling heavily with almost a will of their own, he pulled away from Tim's numb grip, and walked round to the other side of the bed.

And saw.

XXIV

The image existed for only an instant, a flash on the edge of reality like a single frame of something else inserted into a film. An instant was more than enough time to see everything.

Blood. The room was soaked in blood. Too much blood – to the point that it became nonsensical, impossible to grasp. A little blood was a paper cut on your finger, a lot was for a nosebleed that wouldn't stop or a gash bad enough to need bandaging. 'A lot' was . . . so much less than this that it made no sense.

And there, for a split second in the midst of all

that blood, a . . . shape. *A body.* A woman. Someone's mother. His mind didn't want to see it, tried to reverse that terrible comprehension and force it back into the random blur of shapes and colour it had been before, but once understanding kicked in, it couldn't be put back.

Joel gagged and closed his eyes, but the image hung in the darkness behind his eyelids. His muscles went weak, and he had to slam the flat of his hand against the wall to stop himself from collapsing.

When he opened his eyes, he saw a bloody hand-print outlined on the pastel wall, inches beside his own splayed hand. With a kind of mechanical detachment, he noted that it had a much bigger span than his own pale brown fingers. A man's hand. The hand of a killer. The blood was still the bright, primary red of a child's crayon, and only just begin-ning to ooze and blur away the outline of the print. *Still fresh—*

Except not fresh at all – years old, decades old, and printed not on the cracked and peeling paintwork, but somewhere deeper down. Etched into the history of this house, the stain of something so terrible it lingered long beyond the scrubbing away of physical marks.

This was it, he knew without a shadow of a doubt, without even really being aware of what he was knowing. *This was where he killed her.*

Who? Killed who? She'd been the mother of the two dead boys, but who was she to him? He could feel the shape of the events here, but not see the whole picture; presences, without faces or names. Perhaps Tim would be able to pull more details out of the air, wring out more of the story that Joel had been unable to see – or perhaps not. The one thing that had remained constant through every vision and nightmare was the blankness in place of the face of the killer.

There was a further secret here, something so incredibly wrong that even the haunting shied away from revisiting it. Some reason why the identity of the killer was just too terrible for the spirits that lingered in this place to reveal. It was the one thing the ghosts of this house wouldn't tell, couldn't tell.

'Joel?' His sister's voice was tentative. He didn't know how long he'd been blankly staring. Then suddenly she was pushing up close to him, grabbing him by the arm. 'J, did you cut your—? Are you bleeding?' she asked urgently.

He pulled away from her grip, shaking his head even as a twinge from the cut on the back of his hand called him a liar. 'No.' He didn't think a tiny nick from a piece of glass was what she meant.

Sure enough she fell back, looking confused. 'I – I just thought for a moment I saw—'

'You did,' he said bluntly.

Tim let out a sudden gunshot gasp, breath hitching in his throat as he saw what Joel had already seen, and even Cassie had almost glimpsed. He lurched for the door, and Damon grabbed him. 'Whoa, wait! Hold on, you can't—'

'We've got to.' Suddenly finding he could move, and extremely eager to do so, Joel finally wrenched his gaze away from the blood-soaked nightmare before him. A part of him was screaming itself hoarse inside his head, wanting to curl up into a whimpering ball and never come out of it, but somehow that part was locked away and distant, as if the rest of him was watching it from outside a glass-walled room.

He'd always had to be the calm one, the one who stayed quiet and sensible when everybody else was screaming at each other, and somehow even now that controlled and collected side of him refused to let panic take over. 'We have to get—'

'Why? I don't—' Damon talked right over him, but then he interrupted himself, gagging violently as if he'd breathed a pocket of foul air. 'Oh my God. What *is* that?' Clearly he and Cassie were not as sensitive as the younger boys to whatever shadow of events lingered in this place – but they weren't entirely immune to it, either.

There was a huge bang from outside. In the thick, choking silence that had wrapped around them in the bedroom, it was louder than a bomb going off. Damon whirled. 'What the *hell* was that?'

'The door—'

'Back door—' Tim and Joel spoke at the same time. They turned to look at each other, and Joel saw the sudden icy hand of fear that clutched at his guts mirrored in the other boy's pale eyes. He knew this story. They both did. They'd been seeing scenes from it in their nightmares, jumbled out of order and repeated like some kind of crazy clip show. But now . . . now it was all coming together.

And it started in this room. Not with the death, not with the killing, but when the boys came in, and found her. And then . . .

They heard him come in the back door.

'He's in the house!' Tim yelped.

Joel looked from side to side desperately, and then scrambled for the door out into the hall. He yanked it open, met by a wall of wind and rain, as if the storm had decided to come indoors. Lightning flashed, so close that it seemed it surely must have struck in the front garden, and in its aftermath every shadow seemed to move.

'*Who's* in the house?' Cassie demanded, leaping over the corner of the bed to force her way out and join him.

'*He* is,' said Tim grimly.

At the same time, Joel said, 'The killer.' He looked around wildly, but he already knew there was only one place they could go. Upstairs. Up to the loft.

Something made a crash from the direction of the kitchen. 'It's the storm,' said Damon, face pale.

'It's not,' said Tim.

'Can we get outside?' Cassie moved towards the front door, but hesitated as it swung on its hinges and crashed against the porch wall. The swirling storm beyond looked less than inviting.

'We'll be killed if we go out into that!' Damon gripped her shoulder. 'Never mind the rain, there'll be trees uprooted and roof slates flying everywhere. There's no way the outside of this house is in any shape to withstand this kind of wind.'

'Well, it's not exactly safer in here!' Cassie retorted.

'We have to keep going up,' Joel said.

Damon glanced at him. 'That's going to take us closer to the loft, where the haunting is at its strongest.'

'I know.' He grabbed for the banister and set his foot on the bottom step. 'But that's where we have to go.'

They ascended the stairs cautiously, Joel leading the way. The tension filling him was growing steadily, tying his stomach in painful knots. He seemed to feel instinctively where he had to go, what he had to do . . . but he didn't know how it would end. He was following the path the ghost-boy had taken in his final moments – would he even survive its conclusion?

There should have been light flooding in from the window in the upstairs hall: instead, there was nothing but blackness. Joel couldn't tell if the streetlights over the road were gone, or just obscured by the driving rain. Booms of thunder and blue-white flares of lightning came so randomly that no matter whether they were close together or far apart, he was never quite prepared for them.

The hall window had shattered, a spray of glass covering the upstairs carpet. The heavy curtains billowed inwards and ice-rain spattered his skin and clothing, soaking him to the bone in heartbeats.

'Where now?' Damon asked nervously.

'My room's nearest,' said Cassie, feet crunching through the shattered glass as she pushed past him. The door stood open, but as she reached out it slammed, so hard that if she'd been a few inches further forward she might have lost fingers. She spat something that was maybe just an angry sound, jiggling the handle and striking the door with the heel of her hand. Joel wasn't remotely surprised that it didn't budge.

That wasn't where they were supposed to go.

'Joel's—' Damon began, but before he could finish the second door slammed too, rattling the frame and making him leap back with a curse. Joel glimpsed Tim, pale and serious, in the next flash of light from the skies. He didn't even bother looking at the other door. They both knew full well there was only one course of action they could possibly take.

'Up there,' said Tim softly.

'Yeah.'

Joel moved forward and reached for the hatch in the ceiling. He wasn't tall enough to grab it straight away, but with a foot braced against the wall he was able to stretch up and yank it open. The ladder clattered down into the hallway.

Damon's hand landed on his shoulder. 'Joel, are you sure—?'

'Yes,' he said bluntly. He shook the older boy off and quickly pulled himself up, hand over hand. Up in the loft the violent drumming of the rain was clearly audible; the whole place seemed to tremble, and he couldn't help but wonder how stable it was.

The sounds of the others below grew fainter and more distant. The air was thicker; noises muffled, his movements slowed, breaths suddenly a greater effort to force through his chest. Not wholly in control of his own actions, he swivelled towards the cupboard. In his head he could already hear the whispered chant.

If I should die before I wake, I pray the Lord my soul to take. If I should die before I wake, I pray the Lord my soul to take—

Had somebody shouted his name? Vaguely familiar syllables stretched out and distorted until they were meaningless. All the warmth had bled out of the air, and his shallow breaths puffed out in a pale cloud before him. As his feet moved him forward of their own volition, his trainers left footprints in the thin film of frost that was collecting.

If I should die before I wake, I pray the Lord my soul to take—

He could *feel* the presence of the ghosts up in this loft, as surely as if they were solid flesh and blood. He could sense the rising, scrabbling panic, and the building claustrophobia—

Joel's hand closed around the handle of the cupboard door. It burned against his skin, like seizing hold of ice straight out of the freezer. The whispers grew to a crescendo, running through and over each other, decades and decades of repetition swarming in the same place until it was just a hubbub of continuous sound.

*– if I should – wake I – die before I – my soul to – die –
pray the Lord – wake I – take – my soul – before I – pray –
if I – wake, I – should die – the Lord – to take, if – my soul
to – pray the – before I – take – Lord my soul – wake, I pray
– I should – to take––*

He yanked the cupboard door open.

What rushed out to greet him was neither sight
nor sound, but a raw, elemental surge of power that
threw him backwards. He was blasted off his feet,
hitting the floor with enough force to feel the ancient
wood splinter and creak alarmingly. Joel groaned in
pain, letting his head drop back against the frigid
boards.

The loft seemed suddenly filled by a raging hurricane, tearing at his clothes and hair, and he instinctively curled over to shield his face and huddle against
the floor. The babble had grown so loud and so fast
it no longer held any recognizable words at all, just
a ceaseless, overwhelming wall of mind-bursting
sound.

And still it grew louder. And louder, until his whole
body was held rigid with the effort of not screaming, for fear that the pressure would suddenly become

too much and his eardrums would burst. Surely nothing, nothing, could ever be as bad as that incredible level of sound—

Then it cut off. And in the sudden, deafening silence, there was a single, soft crunch, the sound of brittle bone being snapped.

And that was worse.

Joel pushed himself slowly to his knees. His face was numb and wet; he wasn't sure if it was from the melting frost or tears squeezed out by effort and agony. His eyes painted glowing, nonsense shapes in the darkness where they'd been pressed shut so tightly it left after-images.

His mind's eye, however, saw perfectly clearly. He saw the cupboard door thrown open, saw the younger boy dragged out, still panting the same fragment of rhyme, over and over. Saw him thrown to the ground, lifeless, while his brother tried to run for safety and find help.

But the one thing he still didn't see was the shadowy face of the killer. The boy whose last memories he was reliving must have seen . . . and yet, somehow, his ghost was unwilling or unable to remember it, incapable of dragging that last terrible truth into the light.

What was it about seeing his killer's face revealed that had driven him to even greater heights of terror?

Joel rose, and moved cautiously towards the cupboard. The overpowering, malignant sensation of *presence* was gone – it was just empty now. The loft was too dark to see them, but he leaned down and ran his hand over the wall until he felt the imprint of the carved letters under his fingertips. *Michael H.* That little boy had carved his name in here some-time, perhaps during an altogether more harmless game of hide and seek. He hadn't known it was going to end up being a memorial.

'Joel!' His sister's urgent call from below snapped him back to the present. He'd almost forgotten the others were down in the hallway.

He scrambled over to the hole in the floor, and flinched as he felt for the ladder and realized it was gone, snapped loose from its housing. He tried to squint down into the darkness. 'I'm all right. Is every-one OK?'

There was a moment too long of intense silence,

then: 'I think I twisted my ankle.' It was a relief to hear Tim's voice drift up, thin and pained as it might sound.

'Yeah, er, we're OK,' Damon said shakily. 'The whole ladder just— What *happened* up there?'

Before Joel could begin to figure out how to form an answer, something struck the roof above his head, hard. He heard slates clatter down the slope of the roof outside, and a stream of water splattered down into the loft a couple of metres away. He couldn't tell if it was himself shaking, or the building. How much more of a battering could this fragile old house take?

A stressed creak from some unidentifiable part of the building decided him. 'I'm coming down.' Damon, who'd been moving to look up at him, stepped back hurriedly as he swung his legs down through the gap. Too much of a drop to be comfortable with, but there was no time to stop and worry about it now. He hit the sodden hall carpet with a curse, staggering to avoid the glass shards scattered across the floor.

'You OK?' Cassie asked, coming up from behind to touch his shoulder.

'Yeah, I—' Joel winced as a flare of lightning turned the world electric white, and pushed away from the wall. 'We've got to get downstairs,' he said urgently. 'I think the ghosts have— We've set something off – the whole building could come down around us.' He could feel raw, dangerous energy throbbing through the air, making his ears ache and his teeth vibrate. Whatever supernatural chain reaction had been started tonight, he wasn't sure the building would survive it.

He wasn't sure that they would, either.

Tim was pressed up against the wall close to the window, cautiously probing his right ankle with both hands. He must have been partway up the ladder when it collapsed, or else he'd stumbled diving out of its way. 'Can you walk?' Joel asked him worriedly.

'Guess so.' He grimaced, but stood shakily with his brother's help. Cassie moved around to his other side to support him.

'Is it safe to go down?' Damon asked Joel anxiously.

'I have no idea. It isn't safe up here!' As if to accent his words, the shredded curtains billowed and the hallway grew momentarily darker as something huge

251

was thrown past the window. Cassie leaned forward, gaping after it.

'Holy— Was that a *tree*?'

'Let's *go*,' Joel decided sharply, hustling them all towards the stairs. Tim hobbled awkwardly, struggling when he almost tripped over a piece of shattered wood that must have come from the ladder.

Cassie kept a tight grip on his elbow. 'Limp faster, buddy. Don't make me carry you,' she advised, but Joel could tell from the tone underneath it that if she thought she had to, she'd go ahead and do it. He followed the two of them down the stairs, flinching every time he heard something creak or smash below them.

'We have to find somewhere . . .' His mouth was running on autopilot, and he shut it with a snap. Where was there? There was nowhere they could hide from this.

They piled down to the front hall, and found it under several inches of water. Twigs and leaves floated through the dark water in company with scraps of wallpaper and plastic letter tiles. The only illumination came from bolts of lightning outside the swinging front door, the brilliant flashes doing almost as much to blind them as the dark and the driving rain. Joel could see no colours, only outlines and shadows, turning the hall into a forbidding and alien place.

Damon squeezed past the three of them clustered on the stairs, and waded out into the water. He glanced towards the swinging front door, and lightning briefly outlined his face.

'We can't go out there,' he said grimly, words almost stolen away by the chaos of the violent weather. 'That's no ordinary storm. We'd be killed.'

Joel dropped down from the bottom step to join him, hissing at the ice-cold sting of the rainwater, but he already knew Damon was right. There was no way they could go out into the tempest raging outside.

They were trapped.

XXVI

They heard the back door bounce, loudly, and all of them flinched. Joel was suddenly gripped by a mental image so strong he felt split down the middle, as if he was in two places at once. He was standing here up to his ankles in freezing cold water, but he was also out there in the garden, running for his life . . .

'Come on.' He swivelled towards the back of the house as if drawn by magnets. It wasn't even a decision; he was being pulled to follow in the footsteps of the ghost-boy – follow until all the parts that remained hidden had been revealed to him, and the whole truth was laid bare. Whatever it cost him to see it.

Cassie's face passed through a moment of puzzlement, and then cleared. 'The cellar!' she realized. 'We could hide down there.'

Joel hadn't even thought of it – was moving on instincts that weren't even his own – but she was right. 'The last hiding place,' he agreed aloud, and the words resonated with the feeling of inevitability that had settled over him. The last hiding place. Solid earth and brick walls might protect against the worst that the elements could throw, but what good were they against the supernatural? Sooner or later you ran out of places to hide.

Solid earth and brick walls . . . Something nagged at him, attacked what little of his brain that still had room for anything but instinctive reaction, but he couldn't make a grab for it. He sloshed hastily after Cassie through the flooded hallway.

The door to the master bedroom was mercifully now shut. Had he done that? Everything was so frantic and jumbled he couldn't remember. He looked down to guide his feet more carefully – and saw, in the water, clouds of blood drifting up from under the door. The lack of light bleached the liquid of any colour, but he knew without question that it would be the bright, primary red of a fresh cut to the vein.

His sister waded right on through without even noticing, and Tim made a sickened sound in his throat. 'What is it?' Damon asked nervously. Joel didn't answer. He wasn't sure if he *wanted* to know whether it was real enough for Damon to see.

Cassie was already at the dining-room doorway, but he couldn't make himself follow her through that tainted water. Instead he veered left to cut through the corner of the front room.

Something grabbed his foot underwater. Joel yelped, and struggled frantically to free himself before the metallic jangling told him what it was. He kicked the television aerial away with an embarrassed curse. So much for shifting the TV out here to keep it safe. Some of this glass crunching underfoot must be from the screen.

'You OK, Joel?' Cassie called back urgently, hesitating in the next room.

He twisted towards her as he pushed on through the door. 'Yeah, sure, I'm—'

'Jesus, Joel, look out!'

Joel's heart jumped through his chest as Damon dived forward to shoulder him aside. He lost his balance and then his breath as he had to throw up his arms to stop himself hitting the ground face first. There was an earth-shattering, splintering *crack!* as a tree smashed straight through the remains of the front window, dripping branches like groping fingers only inches from snagging his arm.

'Damon!' His rescuer was kneeling in the wet, breathing heavily – had he been hit?

Tim rushed in and tugged on his brother's arm. 'Damon?'

'I'm OK,' he managed to gasp. 'Just—' The fallen tree slid forward ominously, and he gulped and grabbed for Joel's extended hand to pull himself up.

Cassie opened the double doors from the next room to let them through. 'This isn't really a good time to stop and enjoy the scenic route,' she said. 'Come on!' A coughing fit interrupted Damon before he could deliver a sharp response.

Joel stumbled into the edge of the dining table in the dark, and staggered, feeling a flare of pain-sparked nausea as his abused body protested. If they lived through this wild night, he'd be crippled for days by all these cuts and bruises.

Cassie yanked open the kitchen door, and they were struck by a solid wall of wind and rain like a tidal wave. The whole room seemed to have become a vortex of sucking winds that nearly tore Joel off his feet. His sister had to brace herself against the doorframe to stop herself from being bowled over. 'Somebody's got to open the cellar!' she directed.

'I would if I could get through the door!' Damon retorted. All the cupboard doors were banging back and forth. As Joel watched, one was yanked free from its hinges, and went spiralling across the room to hit the sink with a clang. Tins and boxes were rattling around the room, and the floor was awash with dirty foam where a box of soap powder had spilled its load over the tiles. The torrential rain was pouring through the shattered window, drumming on the metal draining board like a crowd of people stomping their feet.

'Yah!' Cassie ducked as a tin suddenly shot out of

the chaos and whirled towards her. It took a deep chunk out of the corner of the door, and Damon swore as it rebounded against his leg.

Joel's attention, however, was suddenly locked somewhere beyond the maelstrom in the kitchen. He stepped forward, unmindful of the winds tearing at him or the barrage of dust and debris that pelted him. His eyes couldn't make out a thing through the sheets of torrential rain and the darkness – and yet some other part of him saw perfectly clearly. Just as it had that very first night.

The ghost-boy, running through the garden. Making his last desperate dash, a futile effort to get over the fence before his attacker caught up.

. . . And you can feel it somehow, you can feel it in the air the moment you step into the house, you don't know what it is but it's bad, it's worse than bad, but Michael doesn't even notice, he's still babbling about that stupid stone he found and he's running ahead to show Mother and you want to yell for him to stop but your voice is thick in your throat and you don't even know what you're afraid of and you want to turn back but you just keep walking—

He was aware of somebody shouting behind him,

but only distantly, both the voices and the howling of the wind crushed beneath the weight of a flood of memories that were not his own.

Screaming, Michael screaming, that's all you can hear, until you step in after him and the sound cuts out, everything cuts out . . .

And you want to pass out, you want to lock yourself away in your head and hide and not see, but you see – you see what he's done, you see what he's done to her, and there's nowhere to run, nowhere to hide, but—

Hide, hide, hide, got to hide, got to find somewhere—

Because he's coming, you can hear him coming, and if Michael doesn't stop screaming—

Tim was beside him, screaming something, trying to pull him somewhere, but he was locked in position, eyes and mind focused on a different place and time.

– Michael's stopped screaming. Michael's saying something, over and over, but you can't make out the words, don't have time to make out the words, don't have time to do anything but try to find somewhere to hide—

Where?—

Up in the loft—

261

Too obvious—

But where else is there?—

He's mad, he's crazy, maybe he won't think to look up in the loft—

And you can hear him smashing up the house, and you know he's going to find you in the end, you know he's coming up the stairs, but still you keep hoping, still you keep praying that he won't find you—

If I should die before I wake, I pray the Lord my soul to take. If I should die before I wake, I pray the Lord my soul to take—

. . . but he still finds you. And Michael's dead, you know that, you can hear it in the way he hits the ground, and your mother's dead, and you're going to die too, but maybe, maybe maybe maybe, if you can only get out, only get outside and over the fence . . . But you can't escape. There isn't any way to escape, there's just—

No escape.

Joel's consciousness slammed back to the current place and time with the violence of a physical blow. And with it came a sudden, white-hot flare of understanding.

Escape. No escape . . .

The running boy had never escaped. The *ghost* had never been able to escape; he'd never left this house. And if he'd never left—

Joel raised his head, slowly, staring unseeing into the turbulent night.

If he'd never left . . . Then he must still be here.

XXVII

'Joel!' His sister's voice roared in his ear, and he came back to himself enough to realize he was being shaken urgently. How long had he been standing there, motionless, as the pieces finally knotted themselves together in his mind? He turned towards her, eyes widening at the sudden inrush of knowledge.

'I know what happened,' he said softly.

'What?' She couldn't hear him over the storm.

'I know what happened!' He didn't wait to see if the words penetrated, just twisted round and charged for the open cellar door. The Wilder boys were huddled there; another lightning bolt lit up their confusion. Tim looked at him strangely, recognizing that some revelation had struck him in the bare minutes he'd stood frozen, but not knowing what. Tim was linked to the ghost just as he was, but he hadn't seen what Joel had up in the loft.

Just a name, carefully carved into the wall at a child's level. Nothing important, nothing significant . . . and yet, the key to the whole mystery. *Michael H.* For God's sake, he should have realized it right away.

The bodies were still in the house. And if they were here, the obvious place to look was that strangely undersized cellar. Except that the cellar was the same age as the rest of the house, so if those two boys hadn't been Sanderson's children, it couldn't make sense that they would be there.

At least, it hadn't made sense until he'd suddenly put two and two together.

He grabbed Gerald's torch from the toolbox in the corner and pushed past the Wilders, descending into the darkness two stairs at a time. The steps were slick with rainwater, ready to send him skidding down to a broken neck with one wrong move, but that didn't slow him. He heard the others chasing in a rustle of clothes and hurried footsteps, but his attention was elsewhere as he scanned the shadows of the cellar, looking for—

That.

Gerald's hammer still lay propped against the wall, where he'd tried and failed to lift it only hours ago. Joel reached for it, barely registering Cassie's gasp and Damon's startled rush of breath. He knew what he had to do now.

The strain on his overworked muscles was agony, but this time he was driven by determination – and maybe something more. He raised the hammer slowly, and the others stepped back from him, suddenly nervous, wondering what the hell was happening, why he wasn't responding to them: had he been possessed?

Joel *felt* possessed. Supernaturally? He didn't know. But he felt like everything had suddenly come together, locked together, and there was no longer any choice or even any thought behind what he had to do. He just . . . had to do it.

He pivoted and swung the hammer high . . . and

let it fall. It bit into the ancient stonework with an audible crunch, brick dust and mortar raining down the cellar wall.

The walls. Gerald had told him the cellar was too small, but it had been *built* small; the wall wasn't a later addition. It had been there since Sanderson had built the house, and Sanderson couldn't have had sons the right age.

All true, and he'd just stopped thinking there, instead of following it further.

Sanderson couldn't have had sons the right age. But Sanderson had married a *widow*. Victoria Hawkins – a woman who might have already had sons of her own. Who might have called one of them Michael.

Michael H. Michael *Hawkins*. Not the architect's sons, but his stepsons. Joel should have realized it long before this. He of all people should have made the connection. And now that he had, it made sense.

A horrible, sickening, *wrong* kind of sense.

He pulled the hammer back, and struck again, barely conscious of where he was or what he was doing. His mind was somewhere miles away – or rather, years ago.

Sanderson and Hawkins. What had he read about them – what had his mother told him . . . ?

He was a rich architect who came to the village to build his dream house . . . kind of obsessive about getting the details just right . . . she had enough of his obsession with getting the house perfect . . . the only strange thing was that she didn't go back to her family in the village.

It was his wife and children leaving him that made him finally go nuts.

But what if it hadn't been that? What if his obsession had driven him mad before they even had the *chance* to leave? What if . . . ?

That blank space in dream and memory, that emptiness where the face of the killer should be. The one thing blocked out above all others, a dark truth too horrible to reveal.

Not some invading psychopath. Not a thwarted robber or a vengeful ghost. Someone who lived there, someone who belonged there – someone who should have been keeping them *safe*.

Why are you trapped here?

Him.

Joel pulled the hammer back, and struck again.

269

Again. Again. Again. He was conscious of the tearing ache in his muscles, but only distantly, like a sensation felt on the edge of drifting into sleep. He didn't think about the weight of the hammer, or the strain on his shoulders, or how long he could keep this up. He simply swung.

And swung. And swung. Until, at last, the bricks collapsed in on themselves, and a dark hole opened onto the pitch-black chamber beyond.

The hammer fell from Joel's nerveless fingers with a clang. He dropped down to his knees, feeling like a puppet whose strings had been abruptly slashed through.

'Joel?' A hand landed on his shoulder, and his sister looked down at him.

'It's me,' he said hoarsely, which should have been a stupid thing to say, but wasn't. He felt as if some other power had been working through him, mechanically swinging the hammer with a determination that went far beyond the reserves of his exhausted body. Now it had deserted him, and he felt weakened by more than just the physical effort.

Cassie reached past him, and tugged one of the

shattered bricks from the edge of the hole he'd made. It crumbled to pieces in her grip, and she seized hold of another. Wordlessly, Damon moved to join her efforts. Joel simply stayed kneeling, too drained to even think of standing as the others worked to either side of him.

He raised his head when Damon made a small sound of dismay in the back of his throat. 'Yeah,' he said quietly. He'd known what they were going to find as soon as he'd realized who the ghosts that haunted this place really were.

Three skeletons, bundled together, looking almost unreal in the way they were so greyed and shrunken and shrouded in cobwebs. Two of them still had the rounder skulls and smaller proportions of children. There was no flesh left to tell the difference, but of course they had been boys, just as he knew the adult skeleton had been a woman. A woman who had been brutally murdered in her own bedroom, hours before her sons had come home to find her dead . . . and met the same fate.

He got slowly, wearily, to his feet. He supposed he should feel triumphant, but all he felt was hollow and tired. Well, they'd solved the mystery; they'd found out what the ghost was trying to tell them . . . and suddenly, he rather wished they hadn't.

Patrick Sanderson had built his dream house, and destroyed himself in building it. But his wife and stepsons hadn't left him – perhaps they'd been planning to, but they'd never had the chance. He'd killed them all, and then sealed them all away in this forgotten crypt before he killed himself. And here they'd stayed, for ever afterwards. Unremembered. Trapped.

Escape. No escape.

Tim stepped forward solemnly. 'It's done now,' he said softly. 'You can go.'

There was no response from the house. Nothing moved, and nothing made a sound. Nor did Joel feel anything with those other senses, the ones he hadn't known he had until the atmosphere in this house had set them ringing like alarm bells. They were alone in the house.

At long last, they were alone.

Epilogue

Somewhere up above, the front door flew open with a crash. It was only with that sudden noise that Joel realized the storm had faded away entirely.

'Kids?' That was Gerald's worried bellow.

'Joel? Cassie?' And their mother behind him, sounding panicked.

'We're down here!' Damon called.

Their parents came charging towards the back of the house, footsteps reverberating overhead. Joel heard his mother curse in irritation. 'Jesus, why am

I wearing these *stupid* shoes—?' The dining-room door banged. 'Kids, where are you?'

'We're in the cellar!' Cassie called up, beaming as relief began to set in.

'We're OK, Dad!' Tim added.

'Joel?' Gerald obviously realized one of them hadn't spoken yet.

'I'm here!'

Anxious faces appeared in the cellar doorway. Joel's mother came charging down the steps towards them, and he noticed she'd kicked off the offending shoes somewhere along the line. 'Oh, thank God you're all right,' she gasped, gathering him and his sister up to squeeze them embarrassingly tightly. 'We were so *worried* – the storm was on the radio, but nobody said it was this bad . . . There were trees down all the way along the road – you must have been right at the centre of it all. It's a wonder the whole house didn't come down around your ears—'

'Oh, *Mum.*' Cassie squirmed out of her grip, looking mortified, but it hardly seemed to matter when Gerald was doing exactly the same thing to his two sons.

'Anybody hurt?' Gerald asked worriedly.

'Tim twisted his ankle,' Cassie volunteered, helping him hobble up a step. Joel wriggled as his mother started trying to brush the leaves and dirt and glass fragments from his hair.

'It's OK now,' Tim insisted quickly.

'Sure it is,' his father agreed sceptically. 'Come on, little guy, let's get you up here and—'

'Er, Dad?' Damon broke in. He tilted his head towards the shattered back wall. 'That wall you were thinking about taking out . . . ?'

Gerald finally noticed the destruction Joel's hammering had wrought, and descended the last few steps to stare at it. 'Damon, *please* don't tell me you thought it was a good idea to start knocking walls out in the middle of a— My God.' He paled dramatically as he saw what lay behind the broken brickwork.

'What's wrong, Gerry?' Joel's mother had given up on picking debris off him, and was now giving the same treatment to Tim.

Gerald's dumbfounded expression might have been funny under other circumstances. 'Behind the wall; there's— Dear God, that's a human skeleton!'

'Three of them,' Joel supplied solemnly.

His mother forgot all about smoothing Tim's hair. 'Are they *recent?*' she demanded, horrified, automatically pushing the youngest boy away as if there might still be time to stop him seeing.

Still shocked, Gerald slowly shook his head. 'I don't know anything about skeletons, but I do know bricks. That wall was no more recent than the rest of this house. Those bones have been there a long time.'

'Then what?' She gripped his arm tightly. 'Did the builders disturb a crypt?'

'I don't think so,' Tim spoke up softly. He'd obviously finally joined the dots and followed the same leap of understanding as Joel. 'I think they're Patrick Sanderson's family.'

'His wife and stepsons,' Joel supplied.

Cassie blinked at him in surprise, then mouthed a silent 'Oh!' of understanding.

'But they were supposed to have—' His mother abruptly stopped and raised a hand to her mouth in dismay. 'Molly said her aunt had disappeared one day without telling anyone she was going . . .'

'Looks like she didn't get far,' Damon said grimly.

Gerald shook his head in queasy bafflement. 'I had heard that the man lost his mind before he killed himself, but this . . .'

'Pretty sick, huh?' said Cassie softly. Joel wondered if she was suddenly reassessing all her petty complaints about Gerald.

'Well, whoever these poor folks are, they've been dead and buried a long time,' Gerald said, making an effort to shake himself out of his gruesome contemplations. 'We, on the other hand, are all still alive, thank God, and I think you kids need some dry clothes and something to warm your insides. How about you all head upstairs and see if you can dig out anything wearable, and then we can drive down to the town and see if anywhere's still got power.'

Cassie gave him a brilliant smile. 'Thanks, Gerald. That'd be great.'

He looked startled, but offered her his arm, and she took it and accepted his help up the stairs without complaint. The others trailed up after them: wet, tired and battered, but together. The house might have come apart around them, but they were all still standing.

Joel was the last to emerge from the cellar, and despite the devastation around them, he couldn't help but smile. He tilted his head upwards, enjoying the cool night air that spilled in through the shattered window.

The Sanderson family might have come to a terrible end, but somehow he had a feeling that maybe, just maybe, theirs was going to work out fine.

About the Author

E. E. Richardson is a twenty-four-year-old cybernetics graduate. *The Intruders* is her second novel for Random House Children's Books. Her debut novel, *The Devil's Footsteps,* was published to critical acclaim in 2005 and her new book, *The Summoning,* is published in 2007. She lives in Essex.

THE SUMMONING

E. E. Richardson

Not everything that comes when it's called can be controlled . . .

Justin has always been curious about his grandfather's fascination with magic, but that doesn't mean he *believes* in it. So when he gets the chance to scare know-it-all Daniel Eilersen with a ritual from one of his grandfather's books, he doesn't think twice. After all, what can go wrong? It's only a bit of old mumbo-jumbo.

His friend Trevor and his sister Joy aren't quite so sure, but Justin isn't planning to hurt anyone. He just wants to humiliate Eilersen. But when a real creature of magic turns up in response to a summoning that was only meant to be a joke, none of them are prepared for what happens next.

A great evil is unleashed that threatens not only their lives, but the very world they live in. As Justin and Joy race against time to undo the damage they've caused, they find that some of the answers they seek are buried in their family's hidden past.

978 0 370 32887 4